Dancing

HELEN FLINT

Not Just
Dancing

MAMMOTH

To Alice, my own teenager, with love.

Author's note: the Home Help Organisation
depicted in this book is entirely fictional.

First published in Great Britain 1993
by William Heinemann Ltd
Published 1993 by Mammoth
an imprint of Reed Consumer Books Ltd
Michelin House, 81 Fulham Road, London SW3 6RB
and Auckland, Melbourne, Singapore and Toronto

Copyright © 1993 Helen Flint

The right of Helen Flint to be identified as author of this
work has been asserted by her in accordance with
the Copyright, Designs and Patents Act 1988

ISBN 0 7497 1409 3

A CIP catalogue record for this title
is available from the British Library

Printed in Great Britain
by Cox & Wyman Ltd, Reading, Berkshire

Contents

Chapter 1

MY FIRST FALSE MOVE

In the end Fran grabbed the form out of my school bag and started to fill it in for me.

'I'm fed up with you not doing it,' she said. She seldom got so naffy with me. 'You'll end up as a mortuary assistant for a week if you don't hurry.'

I suppose she was right. With hindsight I can see how it all started there – I hadn't filled in the form stating my preference for Work Experience Week in time to get a good 'job'. Fran had put down Prime Minister on her application as 'area of work where your interests lie'. Well, it's true, she said – they told us to show ambition.

The thing is I don't want work experience. Surely work is the one thing I'm going to have far too much experience of in my life. What I need is fun experience, meeting boys and growing up experiences.

' "Sex – not yet, but hoping" shall I put?'

'Give it here.'

So I put 'Ballroom Dancing' down and Fran said, 'That's Not work!'

'I'd like to see you say that to my dancing teacher and survive.'

You see, it wasn't so silly as it sounds because I *am* a ballroom dancer. I have been since I was four. I also do Latin American and Disco. I have a room full of medals and a wardrobe full of sequins to prove it. I've been South of England Under Sixteen's champion twice. You've only got to see me walk down a corridor. I know this because Fran herself says, 'Walk normally, won't you? It's so embarrassing.' She, of course, is a skinny bones of a person and shuffles along like an insect.

Well, perhaps it was the Ballroom Dancing, that and the lateness of my application which put me so far down the priorities. All the other lucky girls had already been given lovely jobs like Looking Beautiful in an Insurance Headquarters in town and Making the Tea for Unmarried Handsome Computer Whizzkids, or In Sole Charge Ice Cream Stand on Beach.

Miss Carter called me into her office at break. She is the W.E. liaison officer. She is also a terrible geography teacher and wears Oxfam clothes which some dead person has finished with which she always meant to get dry cleaned. Ditto her hair.

'Well, Geraldine, we haven't been very sensible, have we?'

I didn't say 'speak for yourself Miss Carter' or

8

any of the witty things I thought of later when relating it to Fran – I just said, 'Sorry.'

'Ballroom Dancing indeed! A flippant attitude is not likely to impress any future employers, is it?' So that's what it's all about – impressing people. I should have known. Fran would have known that. If Fran were here, she'd be sweet-talking herself into being the new presenter of *Come Dancing* for one week.

'What does your father do?' she asked me. Hadn't she got that on file somewhere?

'He's a driving instructor.'

'Oh. Does your mother work?'

'Yes. She's a Home Help.'

'A what?' Obviously Miss Carter had never heard of the Welfare State as my dad called it. 'Your mother is one of the few people who still works for the Welfare State,' he'd say, proudly.

'It's a sort of social work, in people's own homes,' I said. Suddenly a sinking feeling came over me – surely not, surely not! Then she said it.

'Well, that sounds ideal, if she would agree. I have nothing left to offer you, but that would fit the bill nicely. I'll phone the Home Help department of the – I suppose it would be Social Services . . .' She began rooting in a box on her desk, ominously happy now. Now that she could with one stroke both satisfy the school and punish me.

'But they die!' I blurted out. I don't know what possessed me. I just panicked, I guess.

'Who do?'

9

'Her clients! They're all ever so old, and they're always dying!'

She laughed. Hollowly. It was what Fran would call 'hollow laughter'.

'They can't *always* be dying, or your mother wouldn't have a job!'

Fran did well. Because of her asthma, she had to be spared any unsavoury environment (smoke filled cabinet rooms in Number 10 for instance) and too much stress (factory work) and so was awarded learning to run a small sub post office with an elderly non-smoking postmistress.

'Well, from humble beginnings . . .' she said. No doubt one day our Fran will be the first female Managing Director of British Telecom.

Mum was thrilled. It seemed she had only invested fifteen years of child-care in me so that one day I could repay her by helping her out for one week. She seemed to find it hilarious that I should actually *have* to do what she said, "for once", and that most of it would be housework. I hadn't lied about the 'social work' bit – it had just been an exaggeration. Actually I know, and this is why I panicked at the fateful interview with Miss Carter, that her work involves unspeakably foul domestic duties done at ungodly hours for those who ought to have passed on long ago. My only hope of salvation is that I'll come down with some dreadful incapacitating disease that lasts exactly one week. Perhaps I could catch Fran's asthma on a part-time basis?

All weekend I did try to become ill. I suppose when you think of all the people who are ill by accident, who, through no fault of their own, have dreadful illnesses, I should have felt ashamed to be wishing away my good health. But I didn't.

Shamelessly I stood in the garden facing the salty wind off the sea with only a thin blouse on (why didn't I catch pneumonia?); I doubled the thickness of margarine on my bread (why didn't my arteries clog overnight?); I gave the snotty child next door a big hug and breathed in her germs (why didn't I get a cold instantly?) and finally, I turned up Madonna as loud as I could and pressed my ear to the speaker. I must admit I felt a bit dizzy after that but when Dad flung open the door and shouted, 'Have you gone mad or what?' I could hear him perfectly, so it hadn't worked.

Late on Sunday night I gave up and agreed to read, lying on my bed, exhausted from all the exertion of trying to become ill, the pamphlet Mum had given me. It looked like the one she'd given me on Young People and Aids or the one called *A family doctor talks to young women about contraception*. She handed it to me just as secretly and left the room. It was called *Home Care for the Long Term Elderly in Dorset*. It had no interesting pictures whatsoever.

When I phoned Fran half an hour later, she suggested I plead insanity.

'How could I do that?'

'You could say you were psychologically unfit to

11

care for the elderly because of your telephone addiction.'

'My *what*?'

'Geraldine. It's eleven-thirty and I'm trying to get to sleep.'

'Sorry.'

Chapter 2

MISS RICHARDSON

I awoke feeling disgustingly healthy – I couldn't even find an inexplicable rash anywhere – so my week as an unpaid slave began at six o'clock on Monday morning.

Mum felt it necessary to remind me every few seconds that we had to leave the house by six-thirty, quietly so as not to wake Dad. Then she insisted that I put a nasty little nylon overall on over my clothes. This was going too far. It was not only nylon, it was turquoise! She should have known I would sooner die than wear such a thing! We argued for some time until Dad's muffled voice told us to 'pipe down'. I won.

There was no time for breakfast because of this discussion, so we headed for the car.

Unlike most families I know, we have two cars. This isn't because of any extreme affluence, alas, but because my father (whose name is Miles) uses his (with the embarrassing pyramid on top saying

Miles Better Motoring which *all* my friends have seen around town, including Fran who said 'deplorable punctuation') for teaching people in all day, so Mum needs her own. Since she has to pay for her car out of her tiny income, it is rather tatty. The one she has at the moment looks as if it longs to be returned to a dump. The passenger door is permanently shut so you have to ooch over the driver's seat to get in. Obviously I go to school on the bus, even when I'm late, it's raining, force zillion winds etc. Even if I had two broken legs I wouldn't want to be seen being dropped off at school in *that*!

Still, today there was no choice. I ooched over, switching on the radio with my kneecap. Radio Solent would be bringing us minute by minute coverage of the Charts — of course this is incomprehensible to my mother. She regards the sound of any music anywhere as an opportunity to talk loudly about something meaningless. If you ask her to 'shhh', she gets angry and shouts her meaninglessness at you. I have learnt that if I really want to hear something I have to shut my eyes and lie on top of the speaker with my ear pressed to it.

So just as Radio Solent were giving a quick airing to Ice Queen, my fave and No 2, she began to tell me all about someone called Miss Richardson. We were driving along the coast road and it was that lovely bit with the saxophone solo. So I only heard *bits* of it.

First of all, she explained (and this ranks with those explanations by the chemistry teacher of what *valences* are, which leaves you wondering who is from the Planet Tharg – you or her?) that Miss Richardson was one of the Long Term Elderly. I didn't bother to ask whether anyone could ever be Short Term Elderly – just old for a while – because I thought the answer might be beyond me, like the valence thing.

What I did understand was that Miss Richardson was always her favourite. I mustn't be put off by the smell. She was a sweet dear. Virtually spineless now as she neared the end of a long, courageous life. Fast becoming an invertebrate: fine for the fishes of the sea, for the amoebae, but not for folk, who must still move through the human air, heavy with gravity. Once she must have scolded her young ladies for arching or slumping – warning them one might want to carry a pitcher of water on that bottom. Posture. She'll approve of *you*, Geraldine. Now that she can no longer walk, she fancies she walked gracefully all her life. This may or may not be true – every ugly old lady boasts of a beautiful youth! And why not? I will. Though I shall have you to contradict me. Miss Richardson has not had the blessing of children.

Blessing? I'm a blessing, am I?

We parked any old how as Dad would say, by the flats. Only old people live here. I braced myself for the smell.

It was a good thing I did. The flat was pitch dark and smelled of decay. Not wet decay like old fish or

15

old living things gone off, but dry dusty decay as when inanimate things start to crumble. Mum called out, 'It's *me*!' rather stupidly.

A clear voice, like the voice of a singer (an elderly female Blues singer) called back through the gloom, 'Isobel!'

Mum must have trotted off through the darkness because at this, a curtain swished open and the silhouette of my mother (short and stubby like a half-burnt candle which was once human shaped) said towards the great bed, 'And look who I've brought with me today!'

Slowly I let my eyes travel towards the bed. I was frightened of what I might see, and also more curious than I ever remember being. Lying under a million covers all in faded embroidery, barely making a ridge under them, was an old, old person. Her face had sunk inwards and her dry, grey hair, like unwatered plants, had died.

'Geraldine!' it said in a surprisingly dark brown voice. I was astonished: how did she know my name? Of course, Mum must have spoken of me. Heaven knows what she might know about me! She was holding out a thin, transparent hand over the bedspread. Mum nodded at me, so I went over and shook it, rather formally. It did seem strange to shake hands with someone in their bed. Especially at my age. Still, at least I am too old to be told to kiss someone.

'You're looking well,' lied Mum.

'Liar,' said Miss Richardson, smiling. In that

smile was a sort of life, I saw with relief, for the white creases of her skin all pointed to her eyes, which were still sparkling bright and grass-green.

So we did the toilet and washing and the breakfast, and all the while Mum chatted away about stupid things – the weather, food, prices – but she showed me how to oil a wheelchair and we threw away some failing plants ('It's your heating here, it's so dry,' said Mum) promising babies from our own porch (we have tons).

In her wheelchair Miss Richardson looked like a female head of the Daleks, an interstellar warlord in her black acetate-silk dress and brushed down steely strands of hair. All the jewellery she made Mum drape upon her only added to this impression, though when I wheeled her to the mirror for 'self inspection' as she called it, she laughed and asked, 'What do I look like?' smiling. Then she added, quickly, 'Don't say anything, Geraldine. Save it for your friends.'

Then came the cup of tea. I didn't really want to eat or drink anything, which is unusual for me since I usually do want to eat everything all the time (my mother doesn't feed me adequately since she never learnt to cook), but to be polite I accepted a cup, and then Miss Richardson said, as if we were just guests of hers who happened to have dropped in for tea: 'Now, let's hear about Geraldine. I am all agog.' I always find my mind goes blank when someone says something as vague as that. Like 'had a nice day at school, dear?' – two hundred and forty-one things may have happened that day but I can't recall one. So I looked at Mum, and she understood the panic in my eyes and started to burble meaninglessly, which was just what was called for, about me.

'How we've searched for the right boy – someone tall enough, of the right *standard* and living locally. We searched all along the South Coast for someone – in Poole, Christchurch, Southampton, anyone almost to replace the brainless Charlene – a hopeless girl but the right shape and standard. Then we heard from Eileen that there was a boy living nearby who fits the bill perfectly. We're going to meet him tonight.' Actually I'd forgotten this myself.

'And the venue? Where will this meeting take place?' Miss Richardson asked.

'At the dance school, of course.'

'Oh, I see,' said Miss Richardson, 'it's just dancing!'

'Yes, what did you think I meant?'

'I thought you had found Geraldine someone to share in life's many trials and tribulations; in short, a husband.'

'What? Would I do that? How could you think that? She's only fifteen!'

Oh, I don't know that it's such a bad idea. In some ways the thought of having to find myself a husband fills me with horror. Who would take me on? Where am I going to find him? Supposing I just never fall in love? All these worries whirl round in me, sometimes at the strangest moments, like in the middle of Christmas dinner.

'But fifteen is the *ideal* age! Despite having reached her full height, I hope – ah, what divine posture you have, Geraldine! – she is as yet plasticine emotionally. She and the young man could mould each other, grow up together, become one in every sense. They could go through those difficult years of late teens *together* . . .' She seemed to be in a rhapsody of her own. Mum stopped her with, 'Well, I'm sorry, he's just a dance partner. That's all.'

'How disappointing,' Miss Richardson said. I felt disappointed myself now, though perhaps that's just because I'm all plasticine inside. Plasticine! The very idea!

Obviously Mum thought it was just one of those strange notions which take hold of old ladies. After all, she was a spinster and could have only a vague idea of what was involved. So have I, come to think of it. On Mum's face was that indulgent look she reserves for me or Dad when we have just said something *really* stupid but understandable, given our ignorance.

I must just say, it isn't what you're thinking – a dance partner. A tall, romantic character in full military attire whisking me off (dressed in a four foot wide white ballgown) through a roomful of admiring diplomats in some exotic foreign city. This is how Fran imagines it. You must meet such lovely blokes at these competitions, she moans.

Lovely! If they aren't short and spotty and thirteen, they're long and gangly and have an IQ slightly below the average hamster. Nothing on earth would induce me even to talk to one of these scumbags, other than technical things like the obligatory 'hard luck' and 'well done' you have to say when greeting other competitors.

Mum was making as if to leave. Heaving on her coat, she held up a duster. We all laughed. It was a solid rectangle of folded fluff glued together with dried spray polish. Miss Richardson, laughing the loudest, suggested we mount it and present it to Miss Fowles as a modern desk sculpture entitled *Home Help bites the dust*. Miss Fowles is head of Home Help.

'Don't let her send me down,' Miss Richardson said as Mum unfolded the timesheet for her to sign. A film like a grey tint of contact lenses misted her eyes. I could see she was on the brink of tears.

'Send you down?' I said. Mum explained, in a whisper to me, that being 'sent down' was her code for being sent to a Nursing Home or an Old Folks Residence. She had often said, not so much as a threat, but rather as a rational statement of fact, that should she be threatened with a Home, she would end her life first. I felt a chill. Then Mum said, out loud, 'Why, what's afoot?'

'I feel it in what's left of my bones. She is scheming.'

'Has she visited?' My mother's face betrayed real worry now, and she said, to me, though Miss

Richardson could hear, 'A visit from Miss Fowles can be the kiss of death in these matters. Just a friendly visit, she says, and the next thing you know it's off my list and into residential care. The speed of the woman! You'd think someone had given her the four minute warning at birth and she's been running ever since.'

'I've not had a visit,' said Miss Richardson.

'You're all right then for now. I'll keep my eyes open.'

Miss Richardson signed in a copperplate flourish for one hour and reached for her pills. I felt awful leaving her there. No one else would come today, unless it was the postman posting leaflets telling her she may already have won a holiday for two in the Dominican Republic, out of her reach on the horsehair mat. As we left, she placed the first painkiller of the day on the back of her tongue.

Please God, may I never be so old. Let me die young in a car crash. And also everyone I love, my parents, my friends. Let none of us ever be alone and afraid like this.

Chapter 3

HUNTING THE ZYLIX

All morning long my Mum and I worked our way through the timesheet. Mr Beaven, the 'new gentleman' with the old heart, rebelled a little and signed only his first name, Hubert. Mrs Longham with the chest exaggerated her own importance and took up two inches with Alexandria, which she thought was her name but I thought was a city. Mrs Stokes, in the Grange flats, was burdened with arthritis and although mobile, could not grip anything any more so we made her a big enough breakfast to last till Supper on Wheels. Mrs Stokes moaned: her pain was the fault of government policies, Miss Fowles' insensitivity and, can you believe it, people bringing their children with them! Me! What's more the doctor said her kidneys were packing up.

'Where to go I wonder? A nice little bungalow in Weymouth? Florida for the hurricane season? Where would a tired couple of kidneys want to holiday?' This was my mother being sarky to her elders! Ha! A wonder to witness. On the other hand, a storm gathered on the face of the old lady. Really, Mum shouldn't joke about kidneys. She was so upset when she discovered that I carry a card willing mine away should I die. I think what really bothered her was that I had faced up to the possibility of my own death, which she hadn't.

I hadn't, actually. Fran made me do it. 'How else can you hope to save *two* lives,' she said. 'One person gets your kidney and another gets their dialysis machine. It's such a good deal. If there's a Heaven, you'll be well in.'

I only did it to please her. Also, I don't think it's likely, if there is a Heaven, that the Keeper of the Gates of It is going to ask, 'Hey, where are your kidneys? Sorry, no entry without them!'

Mrs Stokes checked the timesheet by her watch and challenged four minutes before signing it in her mean little handwriting, precisely hemmed in by the tiny box allowed: M. Stokes. All of a sudden I felt an overwhelming love for this small neat person with her hair in a hairnet the wrong colour who will never have my or anyone else's kidneys.

'See you tomorrow, dear,' said Mum.

'*If* I'm still here.'

'You will be.' It wasn't really optimism, just resignation. I was beginning to understand why Miss Richardson was the favourite. She was in a different class altogether. I don't mean *social* class, but type of person. Not so sorry for herself.

Two more ladies and a gentleman to wash, feed, bless and make sign before we can even think of lunch. Personally, I had been thinking about lunch for nearly an hour by the time Mum said, putting on her coat, 'That's you done, Mrs Peters.'

'Don't go. You've only just come.'

'I must. We need our lunch. Everyone needs lunch.'

Mrs Peters looked distraught and seemed to search about with her eyes for something to hold us with. I was getting wiser now about these 'old folk'. They all had ways to handcuff you. What will it be? Could we help her to the toilet? Make her another cup of tea? Just stay for a short chin-wag? Stay here forever on God's neverending timesheet?

'I've lost my Thing.'

'Your *thing*?'

'You know, my thing that opens things,' and she made as if to heave a boat oar towards her with both arms.

'Oh, your Zylix?'

Now, isn't that a lovely word? Hungry as I was, I couldn't help thinking how brill that word is. Nicer even than Lozenge or Theodolite. The sort of word even Fran would be hard pressed to slip casually into a conversation.

But what is it? Well, old ladies, their grip and/or husbands gone, are sometimes lucky enough to have a substitute, called a Zylix, but unlike the strong arms of the absent man, it is easily lost, being only a nine inch metal stick with an adjustable rubber hoop at the end.

'I last saw it in the bathroom.'

'What did you need it for in there?'

'*Someone* cleaned the bath on Friday and turned the taps off too hard so I had to twist them open.'

'Oh, so it's my fault!' Actually Mum does this at home too – turns the taps off so hard you need a crowbar. It's to do with a fear of flooding.

I began to feel faint with hunger but we found the Zylix, under a pile of towels in the airing cupboard and left before Mrs Peters could think of anything else.

Aunty Bev lived mercifully close and we were there in under five minutes. She was surprised to see me because Mum hadn't had time to warn her, though not Mum, since she expected her every day for lunch.

I find it hard to believe these two really *are* sisters. You'd think they'd have something in common. Of course they do the same job in a way, though Dad says he thinks Mum went into community care when Beverly became a nurse just to 'compete'. Mum says that isn't true but it's typical of men to see everything in terms of a competition. Actually I don't notice them competing, since Aunty Bev has the qualification but Mum has me: somehow it's equal.

Especially since by some miracle I came out looking like Aunty Bev: tall, pale skinned, green-eyed – even my hairline is a copy of hers. So much so that the old old ladies who live with her sometimes think I am *her* daughter when they see me, and people at Competitions assume she is my mum. I don't mind this at all since Aunty Bev is so *glamorous*. Being unmarried and childless, she has never ripened or drooped or flopped or gone to pieces. She spends money on clothes and at the hairdresser. She has style. My mother thinks style is which sort of freezer you choose. When I contemplate my aunt, I vow never to marry. But it doesn't last. Also she herself is determined I shall, and *well*. I'm not sure what marrying *well* means nowadays, but it matters to her.

Everything matters to her — that's the thing. Nothing is slipshod or 'nearly' or just about all right. Everything has to be absolutely right. My friends often wonder at how she manages to keep herself and her house so immaculate when she has such a rough job in some ways — looking after old people. I don't find it odd — I'd find it odd if she did anything differently: that's just her — perfect in everything.

Of course, she is an inspiration to me in my dancing. Even when I win, she says nothing if it was in the slightest bit shoddy. But if I danced really well, and won nothing, as often happens, she is ecstatic!

When Mum told her why I was there, she frowned and just said, 'I hope she won't be too tired for the lesson tonight.'

* * *

26

So, in her wonderful kitchen where everything has a place and lives there, Aunty Bev pointed her graceful and manicured finger at the stripped pine table, and there appeared a bowl of steaming marble smooth potatoes, ham steaks (Mum's cut in half for me) each with a ring of pineapple parading on top, and little Kenyan beans slithering in melted butter. Another *abracadabra* and a basket of croissants appeared — lone horseshoes of flaky bread light as air and graceful as beige swans.

Around the table sat two elderly little sisters, the twins, Edith and Edna. How old they really are is something they refuse to be accurate about: it ranges from seventy to ninety-two. Aunty doesn't mind this — she says no woman should be forced to tell her age to anyone. Between them sat Mr Van Haagen, definitely two hundred-and-four, silently nodding with one arm twisted round his neck, and rocking slightly.

'A clean plate wins a Maid of Honour,' said the Magician. As if you needed any encouragement to gobble up! After a meal here I always feel as if I'm growing, immediately, unlike meals at home.

'Barring Mr Van Haagen of course,' she added.

Of course, how could I have forgotten? Mr Van Haagen's problem is with his throat: he is obliged, so Aunty Bev said, to render all food to a liquid (and beyond, for I once saw him chew milk) before attempting to swallow. This always makes me slightly apprehensive about swallowing myself. Isn't there something deep in the memory bank

27

about chewing each mouthful thirty-seven times to avoid a fate worse than death? You could see him wondering when to dare present to his damaged throat some infinitely chewed morsel. I tried to ignore it. But there he was, counting as usual, silently, each chew: could he allow anything chewed less than fifty times to pass into the danger zone? No. Yes. There, it's gone. One down, eight hundred to go.

I talked between bites (what a luxury when you think of it). Aunty Bev spoke. My mum spoke. The sisters joined in. But Mr Van Haagen said nothing. We all willed him to concentrate and not choke. Please concentrate Mr Van Haagen.

Except my Aunty Bev who, being a nurse, had and would again deal with any choking event with professional efficiency – as if merely saving lives were boring.

Of course, saving *his* might be boring because he is so repulsive, except for his lovely hair, though I should think nurses are used to that. It is really nothing about his appearance as such, just his jerking movements. Never in repose, never still, it tires you to fix your eyes on him for long. The muscles of his face seem to pucker and slacken at random as if he were one of those animated clay models in films which squidge into a ball and become something else, usually a dog, and usually funny. There is nothing funny about Mr Van Haagen though – the moving clay of his face is grey and cold and impossible to interpret. The mind boggles as to what lies beneath those shapeless, zipless, buttonless clothes he has obviously had such a struggle to put on. And while the long white hair is as beautiful as any Sindy doll's, there's too much of it, as if barbering it were a problem.

Then, while Aunty Bev was fetching the dessert (yes, there's even pudding here!), Mr Van Haagen gave up on his meal, sliding the plate towards one of the twins who took half and slid it over to her sister with accuracy and speed, who looked over her shoulder to check that Aunty Bev had not noticed. I whispered to him that he would get even thinner and they even fatter that way but secretly I was relieved that the struggle was over. He smiled and took a deep breath and, bracing his neck against its twisting away from me, he said, in a deep, breathy baritone: 'By Christmas I will have vanished.'

'Oh, doesn't he say the most awful things?' said Edna, or Edith.

'He *always* says awful things,' said her sister, 'but he doesn't mean them,' chewing, swallowing and talking in one rapid movement.

Mr Van Haagen's illness is called Dystonia – such a vile disease with such a lovely name, like some undiscovered Baltic State.

Aunty Bev returned, glanced down at the plates, was not fooled in the slightest, and went to mix Mr Van Haagen a Complan. I know about Complan now – every one of my mother's clients has a box on their shelves. In flavours as various as banana and chicken, they offer a 'whole light meal' in powder form. Mix with water and you have a meal. I'm surprised now that my mother didn't wean me onto this as a baby. Think of the cooking she could have avoided!

'I don't blame *you*, Mr Van Haagen,' Aunty Bev said, glaring at the sisters, whom she did blame. The Maids of Honour were delicious – the sort you can't *buy* anywhere: crisp coconut and raspberry juice outside and a white breeze of buttery something inside.

Reluctantly we made to leave. Aunty Bev was wheeling Mr Van Haagen back into his room when we said goodbye and she beckoned us to come and see what she was making. Not only does she look after three elderly people (for which the state pays her £250 each per week, which Dad thinks is excessive since it is 'the wages of three ambulance drivers') she also invents and creates outfits for me with which to stun the judges at dance competitions.

There are gaudy heaps of medals at home and gaudy heaps of sequined taffeta here in the tiny bedroom upstairs: the link is me. There are strings of pearls in colours no oyster ever dreamt of, piles of floating feathers defying the laws of physics. In real life this always seems ridiculous but at the competitions they seem appropriate, if anything, muted. It is all relative, of course.

She held up a mound of glitter and proudly handed it over.

'Wonderful!' Mum said, not knowing which way

up to hold it. Though encrusted with tiny glass knobs, it felt weightless. Clever Aunty — when dancing, I can forget it. Mum doesn't understand this design tension — the tightrope along which Aunty designs and sews. It must look impossible but feel like nothing.

'Great!' I said, 'it's beautiful.'

'Only for Latin, of course.'

'Of course.' I don't need to try it on — she has a tailor's dummy of exactly my measurements (adjusted six weekly for upward and outward growth-spurts) beside the workbench.

'I wish I knew what he'll be wearing,' she said.

'Never mind,' I said.

Sometimes I wonder (and this wondering brews up in me a mixture of sadness and fear) about why Beverly is the unmarried, childless one. She is so beautiful, and can do so many things. When I was younger, I dared to ask my mother about this but her answer was odd and I've forgotten it.

Chapter 4

OTHER PEOPLE'S COBWEBS

In the car, I switched off the radio myself because Mum was giving me the low-down on the next old dear, and I was a bit interested.

Thrifty Mrs Gaitskill lived in Southbourne Lowrise Sunset Apartments. She will have turned off every means of heating she has because the weatherman predicted 'unseasonable highs', though the weather is no warmer. She has a son in Poole, but they're not talking. She will be Keeping Up Standards and saving electricity, gas, paper, any foil which comes her way, jars, and newspaper, and she will be waiting for Mum, with some dreadful story she is rehearsing even now.

She greeted us with, 'My ceilings need washing.'

'I don't wash ceilings. Even at home I don't wash ceilings.'

This is perfectly true. Mind you, she doesn't even wash sinks at home. Our house is a tip really. Not that I'd want it any other way.

Mrs Gaitskill is a tall person the colour of banana flesh with hair which looks like towering dead lilacs – saving on shampoo no doubt.

'They are a disgrace. Look at them.'

I looked up. It's funny how you do notice cobwebs in other peoples' houses, but never your own. And yet probably our rooms are festooned with the things. This lady must have made a real effort to notice her *own* cobwebs.

'But does it matter? How could ceilings affect you?' Mum shouldn't have asked that – it seemed to be all Mrs Gaitskill required to launch into her story.

'My ceilings are a playground for spiders which drop on my head when I move about, though I can't move about much with my arthritis, of course.'

'Oh, don't worry. Spiders can't hurt you,' said Mum, then adding, I suppose in case I should object, 'except Black Widows and Australian Redbacks which don't live here.'

'That's where you're wrong,' she said and I saw Mum's face drop.

This was the story: she had read of a woman who was bitten by a spider in Spain, and came home with an itchy scab on her arm. After six weeks the scab burst and *millions* of baby spiders hatched out of her arm. The woman died of shock.

Mum pointed out, quite sensibly, that those spiders live in Spain; but Mrs Gaitskill had her there because according to this story, which she knew was true, millions of them were already here and reproducing. Normally Mum said, people who are phobic about spiders vacuum them up, or down rather, but of course she didn't have a vacuum because carpet sweepers saved electricity. If she used a broom, she pointed out, it would simply scatter the creatures all over the apartment, and she didn't want that. She declared that we were both useless and typical of the incompetent people Miss Fowles always sent her, a different one each week of late, and who was this young girl, an apprentice?

'My daughter. Couldn't your son come over from Poole with a hoover and deal with it?'

Mrs Gaitskill scowled, 'You are only saying that to upset me.' Indeed she may have been because she knows better than anyone that family breakdown is the main reason for the existence of Home Help. If families looked after their own old folk, there'd be no need for Miss Fowles or my mum or Home Help.

It seems impossible to me — impossible that relatives could argue so dreadfully that they could never make it up. Not ever. Not even when it was almost a matter of life and death. But it happens all the time. It was probably happening somewhere now as we did some cleaning and secretly put out ten milk bottles (why save the one thing which *is* recycled?) and left soon afterwards, being sure to shut the door so as not to let the draught (and therefore, she warned us, Death) enter.

Chapter 5

DANCING ON AIR

I must have walked through those heavy doors into Paradise over a thousand times. Twice a week since I was four. More often just before a competition. A thousand sightings of that glowing, waxed floor sprung so beautifully – no floor outside Buckingham Palace can match it, they say. At one end is the bar with the record player on it, surrounded by straw and raffia bamboo trees drooping over a speaker the size of a wardrobe. The whole room is panelled with mirrors. You see everyone twenty-three times. It sounds like a weird place but being there is as mundane to me as being in a school assembly hall.

My new partner was standing by a bamboo tree talking to Eileen, and looked round as I entered. Then Eileen moved out of sight and he turned fully towards me. I could hardly make out his features from that distance – the whole dance floor between us, but I could see two surprising things straight away: that he was black and that he was a lot taller than the speaker, and therefore, than me.

Eileen appeared in front of the bamboo tree and beckoned us. Slowly we walked around the dance floor. You mustn't walk on it with outdoor shoes.

He stood there with his hand outstretched for shaking.

'Geraldine, this is Sunil,' said Eileen. He smiled. His face was perfect and beautiful and he was indeed much taller than me – the first of my partners ever to be so. A warm hand slipped into mine and shook it gently.

'Nice to meet you,' I said. Well, what do you say? Fran would have thought of something better, or I might, later. But that's what I said.

'They're well matched,' said Eileen to my mother, who said something about Gold Star.

Mum guided me to a chair to change my shoes. I looked at my shoes – silver, ridiculously high heeled, with a suede sole and a buckle – Sunil, of course, could wear sensible low heeled lace-ups. At an advantage straight away.

I could see Mum was thinking – she had that vague look. Was she wondering about his being black?

'He seems nice,' she said.

'We'll soon find out if he can dance,' I said, standing up on my heels, which makes me almost six feet tall.

Fortunately the music now was a deep-seated

reaction thing in me, like dogs salivating at the sight of a bone. Two bars and my feet move to a certain set of steps. It's just as well: it means I can dance with anyone, up to a certain point. Sunil danced quite well.

Eileen stopped the music. 'Are you shrugging, Geraldine?' she asked.

This might seem like an odd thing to say, but it wasn't. I do shrug. I can't help it. Like all nervous tics, it arrives when most embarrassing. There is a moment at the start of a competition for example, when you have to make a small bow, just a nod of the body really, towards the judges. This was the time a shrug always chose to rear up, as if it had been saving itself for that very moment. Oh, please don't shrug, Eileen would say. I can see why it so bothers people because it doesn't look like a nervous tic, it looks like a gesture – the 'I couldn't care less' one. It's like a two-fingers to the world. It isn't, though. I really can't control it.

I guess I may have been shrugging away during the Foxtrot just then, entirely unconsciously.

'Sorry,' I said to Sunil, 'that's just something that happens to me. I can't help it.' At least I think that's what I said. I may have said 'ooff nar rum oog' because he didn't respond as kindly as I had expected.

'Oh good,' he said, 'I'm glad it wasn't an experimental flourish of some sort.'

One thousand things struck me on hearing him say this. I won't list them all but first, that his voice was rather snooty if you know what I mean – like someone on the telly. Second, that he spoke like Fran (you could do with a dictionary) only he didn't mean well. And third, that he was determined to assume the worst – that I had been trying to impress! Perhaps I shouldn't have been prepared to read into this short sentence so many hundreds of things, but I did.

By this time we were well underway with the second attempt at the Foxtrot.

The whole lesson was a nightmare really. I couldn't seem to take his lead, keep his rhythm, or dance my best. Mum went her usual misty eyed vacant self, pretending to watch, pretending to understand.

At half-time, having a silent drink, Eileen said to Mum, out of Sunil's earshot, 'I don't know what's got into Geraldine tonight – no concentration, even the wrong damned feet!' As I have been dancing since I was four, wrong damned feet is something I am never allowed to do.

'Yes. I think it's Sunil if you know what I mean.'

'No, I don't,' said Eileen in a cross, no-nonsense sort of way, striding off with the strides of a lion – four strides and she was in the middle distance. If Fran could see her walk, she'd stop criticising me.

She put on the Samba music and we galloped towards each other. It was different then. I was in my stride, determined to please Eileen, whom I admire really. Also I wanted to show Sunil that I was a worthy partner. It would be an insult I could not bear if he said to her, quietly but just within my earshot, that he would like her to continue the search for a suitable partner!

So the dancing was different: we moved on the same invisible grid, totally in time with each other, complete concentration bloomed between us. He was a good dancer, better than me even, and we had the 'swing'. At the end of that dance, a two hundred year old man without fingers who makes the tea and sweeps the floor dropped his broom and clapped his palms together.

'Fred might be impressed,' boomed Eileen into the crackling silence, 'but I'm not. Not yet. This is only the beginning. There's a competition on Wednesday I've entered you for.'

This was sudden. Usually she gives me a week's notice. How could she know we'd be able to dance together? Could we really dance together? The important point was that although she had given me no notice, neither was she giving Sunil any opportunity to withdraw.

Thanks, Eileen.

I rolled back towards Mum over the wooden floor and said, 'Competition on Wednesday.'

'Oh, yes? Better tell Beverly,' was all she said.

Sunil, shoes changed in a jiffy and carrying a motorcycle helmet, came and bowed at her. 'Goodbye, Mrs Budd.'

'Goodbye, Sunil.' She frowned at me. 'Such a polite boy.'

That crash helmet! I could read her thoughts: polite boy, but what sort of parents would let a young boy have a motorcycle? Dad had once said that giving a teenage boy a motorbike was slightly more irresponsible than throwing him off the Empire State Building without a parachute. And he always understates everything.

On the drive home I felt strange. A fierce disorder was springing up inside me. Why?

Chapter 6

SIGNING OFF

Our house is a mess. Usually we clear a space on the table and have a snack on lesson nights, standing by the breakfast bar – cheese on crispbread, a gherkin, and a glass of milk. I couldn't eat a thing. A first in history.

'Are you ill?' asked Mum. Normally if I'm not eating, asking for food, or just having eaten, I am ill. So it was a rational question. Fortunately my Dad came home at that moment so I didn't need to explain myself. I felt a shrug coming up.

I couldn't seem to keep calm. Everything was the same, outwardly: the same kitchen, the same parents, even the same food there on the wooden chopping board with the same stain where I spilt half a bottle of precious olive oil (a present from Aunty Bev) and it never went away.

I'm sorry to say my dad wears the most dreadful outfits – a sort of Tintin Goes Punk look he buys from Help the Aged charity shops, his excuse being that if you are his height, tall, and have bright red hair there's no possibility of dressing casually.

When Mum told him about Mrs Gaitskill's ceilings and the spiders living there, he said, 'She could start a small business: Spider Sanctuary, special family rates, no coaches.' You see, even his jokes are dilapidated.

He was just helping himself to some cheese (we are used to foraging my dad and me) when Mum started to wonder out loud why people wanted to learn to drive at night. This makes perfect sense, he pointed out, because in the winter and even now in early autumn most people have to drive home in the dark in the afternoons.

I could see trouble brewing, and I couldn't bear the stupidity of it, the meaninglessness of it. I can't ever bear the slightest disagreement between them. So I kissed them both and went to bed.

I have my own phone. There has to be one advantage to being an only child – this is it.

'Hello, Fran. I've decided to die young.'

'One day in the adult world was that bad?'

'I've seen what it means to be old and I don't want to bother.'

'Well, I had a nice time too. All the world's a post office counter, I've noticed. Reality is parcelled up into grid-sized bits which I lick, stick and hand over.'

Trust Fran to find something interesting to say about anything, however dull. She would probably be able to write a ten page long poem about the postmistress by the end of the week. I pursued my point: 'But try to imagine yourself in seventy years' time.'

'More to the point, our parents in a mere thirty.'

'Oh, yes.'

'Can't see you giving up a promising career on the ballroom dancing circuit to look after your incontinent parents.'

'No.'

'Even your glamorous aunty might get Parkinson's.'

'Oh, don't, Fran.'

'Well, think positive then.'

'Okay, I will. Tonight I met my new dance partner.'

'M or F?'

'Definitely M. Tall enough too.'

'Don't tell me. Spots, shadow of a gerbil-fur moustache, big ears, runny nose, two left feet . . .'

'No, actually he's not *such* a snotrag. And he's Asian.'

'Asian? You mean . . . ?'

'Yes, and quite handsome.'

'Only *quite*?'

'He spoilt everything by criticising me.'

'Nothing's ever good enough for you, Geraldine. He could have criticised my dancing *quite* badly for hours and I wouldn't have minded.'

'I know, but you aren't a dancer!'

'God, you're so *fussy*.'

Dear Diary,
Monday is over at last. Will I make it to Friday? A whole week of this tending to the ungrateful, the irritably old. The long term elderly — it is a good expression because already it seems too long term for me. Competition on Wednesday with new partner — hope only to avoid humiliation since can't practise before then!

Chapter 7

UP AND DOWN

Miss Richardson seemed livelier than yesterday and put this down to my being there. As we lifted her from bed to chair she asked if I would care to dance.

'What do you mean?'

'Be all fizzy and dizzy today. Something to dance about.' This old dear stuck in her wheelchair in a dark flat all day deserved more than dusting. She needed something only I could give her.

'Okay,' I said. Dusting and cleaning were the last things I wished to do anyway though later I'd have to. No one else would give me the option of dancing instead.

It turned out that she had quite a definite idea of what she wanted. First she pointed out a cassette on the shelf and I got it working in an old tape recorder she kept by the bed. It was a Brandenburg Concerto. Then I had to take out a huge transparent scarf from her top drawer. She wanted me to do 'A Dance of the Veil' to the classical music. I pointed out that I didn't do ballet but she just said 'do what your spirit tells you.'

Of course I'd rather have danced to Radio Solent's Top Ten, as I often do to warm up in my room on my own. Lemonade. Funky Gorilla. Boys Boys Boys. Even the Stonk. At first I couldn't think of anything to do, but after a few minutes I guess the spirit of the music did take me over and I danced a bit like Isadora Duncan in that film.

Miss Richardson's eyes followed me everywhere. One movement flowed into the next, and the next. I made it up as I went. She didn't seem to mind. It became easier and easier. Just an old lady laden down with paste jewellery watching me — but you can imagine that I multiplied her into millions of television viewers.

When I'd finally run out of breath and Mum had returned with her timesheet, she clapped and said, 'That has done me more good than all the Home Help in the world. I feel fifty years younger!'

'Good girl,' said Mum, surprisingly. I would have thought she'd object to my doing nothing to help.

Before we went, we had to have the obligatory cup of tea and Miss Richardson had somehow sorted through her wardrobe and thrown out everything but black, because she had decided to be like European old ladies and wear only black things. She showed us a pile of things for me — glittering ballroom clothes, silk suits, blouses.

'Oh, thank you.'

'Let me see you try them on.'

So I did. It was a shock that they fitted. She must have been quite tall once, and fairly slender. And gone to a lot of parties, judging by the amount of taffeta and lace. I'm not sure where I'd ever wear them. Fancy Dress? I'd have to be feeling very brave.

One of the dresses was cream, edged with white birds along its wide, floor-length hem. When Mum had done the final button at the back it became clear to me, in a flash, that Miss Richardson had once been in love.

I looked at her.

Yes, said her grass-green eyes, yes, once.

Later, in the car, I did wonder about whether she was 'the full shilling' as Fran puts it. But then, everything's relative, isn't it? I'm not convinced that Dad's reassuring understatements about the world – like what does one small hole in the ozone layer really *matter* – maybe it's God's keyhole through which he spies on us? – is so sane after all. Mum once said to me that she had noticed that hoarding things was the first sign of Alzheimer's and could begin in infancy with obsessive stamp collecting – giving away dresses isn't *hoarding* at least.

For some reason, I went a bit mad then: I spent the ten minute car journey wondering about Sunil's motorcycle and whether I would ever get to have a ride on it. I imagined sitting behind him going *very* fast, but then having to get off at the end of our road and pretend I'd taken a bus. This strange thought prickled away at me like an itch inside the head.

Mrs Gaitskill didn't answer our knock on her door.

'Being difficult,' said Mum, 'paying me back for my rudeness yesterday.'

'We know you're in there,' I shouted through the letterbox. 'Please come and open up.' No response. Mum banged and rattled the door. It seemed to be bolted, which the elderly are told to do at night. Then my heart began to beat faster. Oh God, had she spoken the truth when last we saw her. Could go at any moment, and had?

'Mum! What can this mean?'

Mum sent me up the stairs to the next flat where I banged on the door. An old man opened it and said, 'What time do you call this? I'm not dressed.'

'I can see that.' Indeed I could, for even in my panic I remember thinking he ought to have put on a dressing gown over his pyjamas before answering the door. But he let me go through the dark stale air of his flat to use his telephone.

'Is it that lady downstairs then?' asked his wife, coming out of a nearby room.

'I'm not sure. My mother is there.' I held in my hand a card with Miss Fowles' phone number on it. That was all I had to do. Phone her. I knew somehow that I must not say *anything* to neighbours or onlookers.

'Miss Fowles? We're at Mrs Gaitskill's and the door won't open.'

'No reply you mean?' Obviously I had not used

the right form of words for this.

'That's it. No reply.'

'Leave everything to me.' She hung up.

At last – some *real* work experience. How many of the others would return next week being able to say truthfully that they had witnessed a death, if death it be? I hoped, sorry to say, that she *was* dead, after all this.

There were lots of onlookers by the time Miss Fowles and the police were in the stairwell breaking down the door.

Miss Fowles was first on the scene. Of course she didn't do any breaking and entering herself, thus making sure everyone, even the policemen, knew she was in control. It was definitely her show. She did this with a combination of body language and the right clothes.

Also her hair, which is miraculous. From the back it reminded me of a raven's wing hat like the ones wicked women used to wear in those old films – a sleek flat one-directional slab of blue-black feather. Her face is so deliberate. Her small features look out with mild surprise on a world which although astonishing, is nevertheless no more than she would expect. She would make an excellent headmistress.

'Stroke, poor dear.' She gave this blessing over the long thin grey-yellow body of Mrs Gaitskill which we found in the kitchen stretched out in a pool of tea gone cold.

Mum found the pulse (the one next to the windpipe) before the ambulance men did because Miss Fowles was watching and it was procedure. I was proud of Mum's efficiency. A policeman was clearing a path for the stretcher to come down the hall.

'How long has she been like this?' an ambulanceman asked of Miss Fowles.

'Only a clairvoyant could tell you that,' she replied, not even looking up from her clipboard.

Or Mrs Gaitskill herself, when she comes round, I thought. She will come round, won't she? It's only a fall, after all.

Even before the stretcher had left the flat, Miss Fowles said, shuffling papers on her clipboard, 'This opens a window, Bel.'

'What?' Mum was giving her that 'how dare you?' look. She meant a window in the sense of an opportunity. We say this in Technology. Obviously, Miss Fowles prided herself on being up to the minute in technological terms.

'I have a young lady sent home Terminal in Exmouth Road.'

'Oh no,' Mum said, 'please. I've got the girl with me.' But I've heard enough about the Foul One to guess that 'please' would get no one anywhere and also that Exmouth Road would be *now*.

I can't dwell here on the horrors of Exmouth Road, whatever they may have been, because Mum left me in the car outside.

'You'll thank me for this one day,' she said. It's funny how many things I'm going to have to thank her for. I'll have to set aside about a week of my adulthood just to say thank you for all the things I didn't understand at the time. Also, it was so cold out in the car I had to chatter in Chinese to myself, you know the way you say *hong chong fueng* when the bath water is too hot or cold.

After twenty minutes, Mum came out looking very relieved, and drove at top speed towards the Portman Estate, and the joys of Miss Eaton.

Joys because there is nothing whatsoever wrong with Miss Eaton except extreme old age. The sort of old age people congratulate each other on. At least if the local papers are anything to go by – there's always some old dear who is celebrating her 105th birthday and puts her longevity down to having avoided everything fun during her whole long life (eating, drinking, falling in love . . .).

'How old is she?'

'Only she knows. When she needs a home visit from a doctor she is one hundred and three, but when the RSPCA come about her seventeen dogs, she is only eighty-five and well able to exercise a few animals.'

Miss Eaton was tiny. She barely reached my waist. Obviously the dogs had sucked size out of her, for they were huge, gruesome creatures, all mongrels, all smelly, and the house displayed evidence of canine occupation (doggie-bowls, doggie-towels and doggie-beds) everywhere.

When we had cleaned, we sat and had our tea on her window seat. It was sitting there in that vast window seat overlooking one of the finest gardens on the Estate that I realised that people can have an impact on the future, even humble people like Miss Eaton and myself.

I noticed a splendid oak tree in the middle of the garden. She was eating sandwiches (which is all she ever eats, attributing her longevity to this and avoiding men in favour of dogs) and I said, 'What a lovely tree,' or something silly like that. She stopped chewing for a moment (are they her *own* teeth I was wondering) and said, 'Yes, but I wish I hadn't put that acorn in the very *middle* of the lawn.'

'You *planted* it?'

So it came to me that Miss Eaton had changed the future and watched it come true. It was a shock – that huge tree, now so tall that it blocked light to several gardens, planted by this small woman, no doubt smaller and smaller with the passing years.

'Yes,' she said, 'Down went the seed, up came the tree, down went me. All up and down is life, isn't it?'

Mum laughed.

'Er, yes,' I said, 'it certainly is.'

I want to plant a tree. But then I'll have to stay alive for a hundred years just to see it mature, which might be a struggle. Especially since I'm planning to die young.

Chapter 8

THE TWO FALLS

At Aunty Bev's it was very difficult to keep quiet while Mum described Sunil to her. She missed out all the important things, like his being rather arrogant, obviously a Grammar School boy, etc. She only said that he was tall enough, the same standard as me, a polite boy and Asian.

'How exotic,' Aunty Bev said. 'That's good – it'll be a first for the County. I wonder what colours he'll wear on Wednesday? I must phone his mother. I made jade.'

'How do you know about Wednesday?' I asked. Eileen had phoned her. Warned *her* but not me! 'And please don't phone his mother.'

'Why not?'

'We don't know them. I don't want them to think we're fussing!' Obviously growing up entails forgetting what embarrassment is!

'Fussing!' Aunty Bev looked astonished. After all,

she does spend most of her life fussing about something, I guess. It's her hobby in a way.

'Jade goes with anything nowadays, doesn't it?' said Mum, trying to smooth everything over. She's got a point – gone are the days when you had to be colour-co-ordinated with your partner.

Aunty Bev just gave me her tolerant look, the one *we* reserve for when Mum says something really stupid, excusable on account of *her* ignorance. Oh, see how I am pulled between the two of them!

'One of our ladies nearly died today,' I said, to change the subject.

I haven't been to a funeral, but most people my mother's age might go to a funeral every five years or so. However, Aunty Bev and my mother, because of their jobs, go to lots of funerals. So I suppose it's no good feeling gloomy about them. I wasn't surprised when Aunty Bev offered to come and swell the numbers at any funerals, should the worst happen. She has a wardrobe of natty black numbers. So does Miss Richardson, I told her. Mum has no black: she wears brown to funerals, much more apt I think because it looks earthy rather than swish.

The thought of Aunty Bev gracing a funeral with a swish black outfit (how would Miss Fowles top that?) made me smile.

There were baked potatoes, fromage frais with olives, and apricot delight to follow. The twins had done one of their 'jobs' on the table, which means they had laid it with a combination of their odd artwork. It was for my benefit so I oohed and aahed over it. Actually, it is astonishing – it's a sort of basketwork. They make corndollies and table mats and even straw hats out of dried grasses which they send away for from catalogues. They once demonstrated to me how they made these intricate mats and I could see why it was the ideal hobby for twins – it required four hands to do it!

The table was laid with about two dozen raffia and grass mats, each one unique and beautiful, some star-patterns, some flowery, some abstract.

'It's lovely, twins. Gorgeous,' I said.

'Specially for you,' said one of them.

I must say people often *tsk tsk* over the exploitation of the elderly in this town, and I suppose there are some who aren't properly cared for, but you couldn't have better fare at a ten-star hotel than here. I shall be noting this in my Report when I write it.

As we drove through Boscombe I found myself worrying about why we had been unkind to Mrs Gaitskill shortly before her fall and yet felt no remorse now that she was gone. This seemed suddenly like sacrilege, even though she wasn't dead – just off our list.

Who else would have given Mrs Gaitskill the time of day? We weren't the only ones cruel to her – just possibly the last ones outside the hospital which would now gobble her up forever.

Down near the pier, they were putting away all traces of the grockles (our word for tourists). The town was changing its skin from seaside resort to old folk's last resting place. Dead beds of red and white begonias: everyone knows red and white means death. And the flapping of tired deckchair canvas, ripped and whipping in the wind reminds me of something sinister which once happened to Fran down here.

Fran's real name is Fancy. As if that's not bad enough, her surname is Goode. Yes, Fancy Goode. Her father thought this a good joke. And before Fran was old enough to drop the Fancy and become Fran, kids used to tease her about this name, especially since there is a shop of the same name not too far from Boscombe pier which sells buckets and spades etc.

Her mother was busy with her younger brother on the beach and Fran (I imagine her much as she is now: bespectacled, weedy, but even smaller and paler) couldn't bear any more teasing and went to hide. She ran up the stone slope by the cafe and found a doorway. She didn't know – how could she? – that she had stumbled into the men's toilets. Nothing terrible happened to her but since she had her eyes shut (to be invisible) she was frightened when someone lifted her up and carried her back to her mother, who was furious.

She thinks now it was Beach Patrol – life guards who cruise the beaches looking for trouble. Now she says, 'if ever I have two children, I shall love

56

them *equally*.' Being an only child, I'm not sure what she means.

Illegally down the access-only road we went, for a short cut home, and found a stall still selling Dorset fudge. What luck. I persuaded Mum to buy some and she had an idea.

'Let's drop in on Miss Richardson and share the fudge!'

'Yes,' – this would (somehow) make up for any lack of kindness towards poor stricken Mrs Gaitskill. Mum must have read my mind. She turned the car around, grinning.

Miss Richardson was on the floor in her sitting room, crying. 'I'm all right, Bel, I'm all right. I've just had a little fall. Ever such a little one. Please don't take any action, don't do anything rash. Let me explain. Please. Help me. Bel, you're a friend. Don't tell Miss Fowles please. I just rather unwisely thought I would transfer some geraniums to the windowsill for some light and I . . .'

'Too perky for your own good I see.' We lifted her back into the chair and I felt fully restored in the eye of Heaven.

There didn't seem to be anything broken (Mum checked) so we put the kettle on and jollied her round with talk of fudge.

I made tea and we ate the fudge entirely (I think they must be her own teeth) and spoke of the sort of things you do when visiting a friend, as if there had been no fall. Mum told her about Sunil. Miss

Richardson looked over at me meaningfully. I shrugged. Twice.

Somehow it was a false sort of atmosphere which I couldn't account for. It was almost as if this fall made some sort of difference in the relationship between my mother and her favourite lady. As if Miss Richardson had let my mother down in some way – as if it were her *fault*.

I understood this all too plainly when we went out to the car.

'I'll have to phone Miss Fowles,' said my mother.

'No! Why? You promised!'

'I didn't promise anything, and she knows that.' I couldn't believe it. My mother was about to turn Judas on a friend, to put into the hands of the Foul One an awesome power: the power of life and death.

Judas started the car and headed for home. She switched on the radio. I switched it off. Oh no – we shall have no distractions.

'All right. Supposing I do nothing, and there are invisible internal injuries there which gradually get worse so that she dies in the night? Whose fault would it be? Mine.'

'You are a coward,' I said.

'You don't understand, Geraldine. You haven't had the training. Always report an accident, however minor, and you are covered.'

'I'm totally fed up with being told I don't understand things. I understand Miss Richardson better than you do. She'd rather die in her own home than go to a Residence.'

'What she wants and what she needs might be different things,' she said.

'Are you God?' I screamed. I felt myself losing control now.

'No, fortunately Miss Fowles is, though.' She laughed. I laughed then too. I felt so overwrought about this it was ridiculous. Compromise. Fran has taught me this – when adults are being really horrendously stupendously stupid, compromise. They like it. They fall for it.

'Then could you tell her about it but make out it was hardly anything at all?'

'What do you mean? Lie?'

'Not exactly. You know how Dad always understates everything, so that a flood is "trouble with the damp", my appendectomy was a "little medical upset"? Like that.'

She did seem to be considering it while we entered the house. Or considering something. She sat for a while in front of the phone. I hoped she wouldn't phone at all. I willed her not to.

She phoned. I heard her telling Miss Fowles that Miss Richardson had *bumped* herself slightly while manoeuvring with the toilet. It sounded so plausible, but then she frowned and listened. 'Let me deal with it,' she said into the phone and then after a gap, 'yes, there's no hurry, she'll last the week. I'll do everything.'

'Well?' I was on tenterhooks.

'The Foul One knew what had happened as surely as if she'd been there. I should have known. She said she was not surprised and had been waiting for this, and that she would "have to go then". See, understatement did not get me anywhere.'

'But you said you'd do everything.'

'I know. But what?'

'We'll have to find somewhere else for her to go.' Logic, isn't it, just logic?

'You make it sound so simple,' she said.

I always thought Mum's work was menial. I imagined her slopping out and dusting and dealing with incontinence and other horrible things. But I never thought there were real issues like this. I never thought anything important could happen in such a lowly job.

Of course, Mum can't reach any important decisions on her own. So we headed straight back to the car and Aunty Bev's. She would know how to solve this one.

While Mum told her all about Miss Richardson and her fall and the phone call, I wandered about in the kitchen, unable to sit down.

'Why don't you sit down?' asked Aunty, crossly.

'I can't,' I said. It was true. My sitting down apparatus had failed me. Perhaps like Mr Van Haagen I would have disappeared altogether by Christmas, on account of an excess of anger?

'What about sheltered accommodation?' Aunty asked.

'No money. The flat is the council's.'

'Why is she so against nursing homes? Pine Lodge is okay, or Hengistbury.'

'She wouldn't go on a waiting list so it would be Pine Haven.'

'Oh, God!'

'And anyway, she has a terror of being institutionalised. Apparently her best friend, a teacher, went into a home and became a cabbage almost overnight. Stared at a pot plant all day and couldn't remember her name.'

'Probably Alzheimer's.'

'Yes, perhaps, but Miss Richardson is terrified and I know she'll do something silly if threatened with it.'

'Very few very old people actually do take their own lives. Tragically, it is mostly young people who try to do that.'

'But I think she might.'

'Then perhaps that is her own choice and we should respect it. I've come to think that old people who are not senile often know what's what.' Aunty Bev can be hard sometimes; it's only her nursing background that makes her think like this.

'What's what? What does that mean? We have it in our power to prevent her feeling desperate enough to consider suicide!'

'We?'

'Well, I'm sure something could be worked out. Between us.'

'Listen, Bella: I try to keep my distance with the

elderly. You have to. I'd expect Geraldine to get a bit involved – it was what I feared. But *you*? You ought to know better. Stand back and let it happen. It's fate – what will be will be.' Then she got up to collect the coffee.

Mum looked at me and frowned her puzzled frown.

At the other end of the kitchen Aunty was pouring some coffee into a spout beaker for Mr Van Haagen, and Mum said, 'I was wondering if she could come here.'

So that was it – that was her plan!

'Here where?'

Mum gazed through the archway into the hall, beyond which was Mr Van Haagen's room, the dining room, the sitting room, and the front door. There was also a small toilet under the stairs leading up to the bedrooms where the twins slept amidst piles of dry, sorted grasses, the room where Aunty slept, and the tiny sewing room where my dresses were born.

'What do you use your dining room for?' Mum asked. It was one of those loaded questions like the ones teachers ask you – 'What do you think *you're* doing?' – which hardly require an answer.

Being Aunty Bev's, it was a beautiful room: the curtains were Liberty Print, the table was round and the mahogany so polished it reflected the scrollwork on the ceiling plaster even on dull days. A piano stood in one corner, and there was a bureau with a million little pigeon holes and an inlaid roll-top. When I was little, I remember being allowed into it at Christmas and on special occasions, when the table was set with platefuls of wonderful small tasty things, fruit and flowers. But now I can see that it is Aunty's one link with a splendour nothing else in her life (except possibly the cars) can give her. That room is perfect, beautiful. Neither the twins, nor Mr Van Haagen, nor sticky-fingered children may ever enter it. It is a sort of shrine.

And Mum had questioned the *usefulness* of it!

Aunty didn't answer. I sat down, finally, on the end of the bench. They stared at each other for ages. I could feel a solid thing inside me, like a bomb, ticking away.

Chapter 9

THEY MAKE UP THEIR MINDS

It was as if I wasn't there, almost. I was there. I was sitting at one end of the pew, admittedly further from the table than either of them. But this goes way back into the clouds of history – playing on the floor between them while they gossiped shamelessly, colouring in something while they criticised life, trying on ballroom dresses while they spoke of mysterious hot flushes. Their sister-hood always seemed to take precedence over my child-and-niecehood. Their closeness disappears me.

In a way, I don't mind. I am in a world of my own anyway. So much is going on inside me, ticking away, that nobody knows about, it is little wonder I never get much done. Daydreaming will be your downfall, my dad told me once, just after he'd read a school report. Perhaps it's true, but how can I help it? I don't *decide* to daydream.

* * *

After the centuries of silence, Aunty took a breath and spoke.

'Nothing any more. I used to entertain in there.'

Mum didn't seem to notice the sadness of this. She just smiled and said, 'Fine, then we could move in a bed and stuff, and Miss Richardson could become your fourth paying guest.'

That's what Aunty prefers to call them — paying guests — rather than the horrible Long Term Elderly the Home Care organisation calls them.

'Hang on a minute. Not so fast there. That's a lot of extra work you're landing me with, Bel.'

'I know. But we'll help, won't we, Geraldine?'

I started.

'Yes, of course,' I said, hardly knowing what I was agreeing to.

'Oh, will you?' asked Aunty. 'How exactly will you help then?'

Mum jumped up and said, 'We'll take Mr Van Haagen off your hands more. We'll start now by taking him to the beach before tea: he'll love that.'

Aunty smiled and looked round at me.

'I suppose,' she said, 'if it doesn't work out, I can always get rid of her.'

'But you won't want to,' I said, 'she's a lovely person.'

There was nothing to read on her face except possibly a recipe floating down from the enormous delicious Meals' File up in her brain's top cabinet.

As Mum was taking Aunty's car keys down from

their hook by the back door, she said, 'Satisfied?' — as if all this were my fault! What have I done? I just sat invisibly by, while they made up their minds.

Chapter 10

GROCKLES' GASP

I always experience a rush of excitement in Aunty Bev's cars, for she always has a nearly new German car with a leather interior and doors so quiet you wonder whether they have really closed. The engines purr quietly, rev counters count and the cockpit-like dials rotate. She has a passion for these cars and she is not ashamed of the extravagance, though Dad says it is no extravagance because they don't depreciate as fast as his Ford Escorts do. I think he too would buy such a car if he could.

When we go anywhere as a family, Dad always drives. I love to watch him driving. Dad never has the radio on: driving is not an occupation like knitting, he says, requiring only half the mind. Good driving is like proper tennis – you do it and if you mean to do it, do it well.

And like the audience at a tennis match, I sit admiringly in the back, knowing that he is finding the obvious simple solutions to all our problems while he drives. For often at the end of a long drive he stretches, shakes his head as if re-engaging his brain, and utters some profound wisdom. Like 'Don't worry — somehow we'll find the money for Geraldine to go to France.'

Mr Van Haagen settled his long white hair into a pleat along the side of his head against the headrest as if he had already worked out the one comfortable position to be in in this car. This is why we aren't in Mum's car — there is no such place. His continual spasm and jerking was distracting; it was like having a fidgety child in the car, but one you can't ask to keep still.

'Where to, I wonder?' He spoke so softly I could hardly hear him. I suppose his accent is still slightly Dutch, though you don't notice it. Someone once told me that if a French person heard a Dutch person and an English person talking, they wouldn't be able to tell the difference. It's just a slight curl in the vowels really.

'The beach,' Mum said. He didn't ask why. I knew he wouldn't. He only ever seems to say one thing and then falls silent for another hour. It is as if, and this may be an actual symptom of his illness for all I know, talking tires him out and has to be carefully distributed in his life. The twins often claim to know all about him but you do wonder if they're just making it up or not. They said for instance that he had once been shot at by one of Hitler's bodyguards, but it's hard imagining him telling *them* that!

Watching Mum drive, from the back, is not nearly so bracing. In fact, I often count to ten to calm myself as she races up through gears 1 to 4 just to be done with it, whether or not any other factors require it. I wouldn't find this so worrying if Dad hadn't pointed it out so furiously every time she has to drive him anywhere.

We made it to the beach.

To me the beach is one of the few free places where you can gather to meet people. The ice rink costs money. The swimming pool costs money. But this is free, other than the odd ice cream, which you can do without if need be.

But you have to have a reasonable body to expose in a swimsuit, that's the trouble. It's okay for me because I have what Fran calls the acceptable late twentieth century shape but she doesn't. No bust. As a result, she will never never come with me to 'parade' on the beach. This is worse than it sounds because I can't parade on my own. Everyone knows you must have a friend with you, if only to have someone to swap criticisms of boys with. Also it's safer. Then you can always say – No, not now, I'm with her.

Mum parked at the top of the cliff at Grockles' Gasp. It's a strange place where the shape of the clifftop is such that when you stop and look down, you have the sensation of being at sea, or at least one hundred feet in the air over the sea.

Mr Van Haagen looked and gasped. Mum turned

and smiled at him. 'You like the sea?' she asked.

'Who doesn't?' he said. It's true — whoever visits us, they always want to look at or touch the sea. It seems to be a need which all humans share.

Obviously there was no way we were going to get down with Mr Van Haagen. There just is no direct way down to the beach for it is several hundred feet below the level of the town, so a walker has to weave down like a skier on the zigzag of a steep slope seeming to be sometimes further from the beach level, sometimes nearer to it.

How we would get his wheelchair down is unimaginable: you would need strong brakes. Or gears. Dad says the ideal driver (himself?) hardly needs use the brakes if he is using the gears properly. But a wheelchair has no gears.

Mum said, 'Would you like an ice cream?' to Mr Van Haagen.

'Yes,' we both said, together.

'It is the one food my throat likes,' he added.

She went into the Clifftop Cafe (a strange white flat-roofed building with round windows, always empty at this time of year) and bought us each a cornet with a flaky bar of chocolate stuck in it. Technically, I'm not allowed to have ice cream. 'One ounce of flab and I'll scream,' says Aunty Bev, despite the adjustable dummy in her sewing room. But today all the rules seem to have gone!

Conspirators in evil!

'We've got something to celebrate,' Mum said to me. But since Mr Van Haagen was right there, she just winked. For some reason, it wasn't right to mention Miss Richardson in front of him.

So we sat there with the windows open, eating our cornets, watching in the distance small boats bobbing on the surprisingly rough sea. It was low tide and acres of sand round the bay were dotted with men in anoraks sweeping metal detectors before them like naughty invisible electronic dogs. From time to time they stopped and dug a small hole with a trowel.

When we delivered him home, we stood watching Aunty Bev feed everyone in the kitchen, hoping to be asked to stay. For nutritional reasons. Far from having spoilt his tea, the trip and the ice-cream had increased Mr Van Haagen's appetite, for he held up his plate for seconds when Aunty Bev said, 'The beach seems to have done you good, Mr Van Haagen.' Our first success!

'Has he been to the beach then?' asked Edna. At least, I think it was Edna.

'Who took him?' asked Edith. Now Aunty Bev looked uneasily at Mum – no one had foreseen this resentment.

'Curiosity killed the cat,' said Aunty Bev finally.

'Yes, but my sister wants to know who took him because she is very fond of the beach,' insisted Edith. They always do this apparently. Aunty calls it 'ganging up separately'. Obviously they are *both* very fond of the beach because they are really one person with four hands, but it seems more assertive to stick up for each other like this.

'I did,' Mum said, 'and we're just going. I must cook something at home. Perhaps next time we'll take everyone. All right, Edith?'

'Yes, only I'm Edna.'

'Sorry.'

'She's not Edna, I am.'

Mr Van Haagen was guffawing so much he began to choke. Everyone concentrated on the choking. He stopped abruptly and breathed again. I often wonder if *he* can tell them apart, and why he seems to *like* them so much.

'It's quite all right. She gets confused,' said Edna, or Edith.

'Yes, don't we all?' said Aunty Bev. We went home.

Dad had made a big effort to be early, presumably because of the talking-to Mum gave him yesterday, and had found the house empty.

He was able to inform us that he had added water to a sort of grey vegetarian shepherd's pie mix for us. For him (and, to be fair, for my mother also) this is major cooking.

We were eating in front of the television when Aunty Bev rang. Mum answered it. I picked up the sitting room phone without Dad noticing and listened in.

Even if Dad had noticed, he wouldn't have said anything. It's not that he isn't strict with me – he is. But only at the last minute. I think because he doesn't see me much, he tries to be the nice guy on my side, but there's only so much he can take, so after a while he'll lose his temper and become strict. Growing up, for me, is learning to foresee when this moment is about to arrive. Predicting it.

At the moment he was just sitting there, feeling indulgent towards me. So I took advantage (you have to, if you can!) – I had to, they might talk about me.

The only thing I did discover was that Aunty Bev obviously meant to hold Mum to her promise of taking Mr Van Haagen off her hands during the day, and suggested we could start with Swimming for the Disabled at the local Leisure Centre tomorrow. So would Mum come round after Miss Richardson, bringing Miles' swimming trunks?

When I'd carefully put the phone back, Dad was trying to speak to me. He was asking about how my Work Experience was going. I did think of trying to say something, either about Miss Richardson, or Mrs Gaitskill, but didn't know where to start. Mum solved it for me by saying, as she breezed back into the room, 'Fine, she's a great help.'

In the privacy of my own room, I was nearly too tired to undress. I dialled half Fran's number and stopped.

Dear Diary,
Tuesday has been even worse than Monday. Mrs Gaitskill (the one with the spiders) fell in the night –

was rushed to hospital. Then Miss Richardson fell and Mum and I fell out about whether or not to tell the Foul One. She did. We have promised to take care now of Mr Van Haagen so Aunty Bev will feel able to take Miss Richardson on. Oh God, everything is such a mess! I wish I was back at school! I never thought I'd think that.

Chapter 11

BEING READY

On Wednesday, the day of the competition, Mum woke me at dawn with, 'Where's that horrible puzzle of York Minster?'

Both she and Dad assume that anything dwelling in my room is 'lost'. They even say, when something is missing, 'Well, at least it isn't in Geraldine's room,' meaning that one day they'll be able to find it: it isn't lost forever. This is totally unfair, since my room is organised but on a system they aren't intelligent enough to understand.

Since the puzzle in question was an unwanted Christmas gift (from the twins), it was on the top of my wardrobe, covered in dust. I got it immediately, to prove something, and almost threw it at her.

'What do you want that for?'

'You'll see.' She was also holding a pair of Dad's swimming trunks. These I understood, due to my telephone espionage, though I didn't say anything.

We set off – Mum with Dad's boxer shorts in her

pocket and I with a large jigsaw puzzle box under my arm.

I entered Miss Richardson's flat fearfully. Mum had said she would 'know by now'. How? By telepathy? She was right. Already piles of things were all over the sitting room with labels saying 'Oxfam' and 'sell'. How she managed to do these things was a mystery to me.

'I've finally faced up to reality, Isobel. I have to go, don't I?' She didn't seem to be holding Mum responsible! Or me! 'Life is catching up with me.'

'Yes, but the question is *where*, and that's what I'm working on now. Don't worry, it will *not* be an institution. I am buttering up my sister who is a trained nurse.'

So that's what she calls it, buttering up!

'I'm not worrying. It couldn't have come at a better time – I have two champions now. Therefore, I fear no evil. By evil I mean Miss Fowles of course.'

'But before we celebrate, there is one more hurdle I have to tell you about. The Visit.'

'What do you mean?'

'It's compulsory – you have to have a visit.'

'But if I'm going, why does she need to visit?'

'If, in her opinion, you need residential care with nurses, I can't settle you in a house, say with my sister. But if she thinks you only need sheltered accommodation, we're all right.'

'Oh no. I'm still at her mercy then. I thought I could sidestep her.'

'Not quite at her mercy. I have thought of a few

76

plans and won't let her visit you without me.' She smiled. 'Without us I should say.'

'My Guardian Angels,' she said. Or hangman's assistants, I thought, depending on the outcome. The main thing was to make sure Miss Richardson was *ready* for the visit.

Being ready, Mum explained to us both, consisted of three things guaranteed to squash the suspicions of Miss Fowles. First – any burglar could use a credit card and get into the flat; she must use the bolts and chain provided.

'But what if I should need anyone?' she asked. 'How would they get in?'

Mum obviously didn't want to go into details here so she just said, 'The ambulance men or the police can *always* get in if they need to, but it won't come to that.'

I was thinking of Mrs Gaitskill, of course. They had all thought nothing of breaking down a perfectly good door. I was surprised; I had thought they'd pick the lock. I hate destruction. It makes me feel ill.

Secondly, she must fill her appointment diary which she kept by the telephone full of imaginary visits and outings, to give the impression that she was busy with her two zillion local contacts.

'But I haven't any,' said Miss Richardson.

'Beside the point.'

Thirdly, she must have about the flat evidence of some hobby. This need only be a half-finished jigsaw puzzle, but it must be indicative of some ongoing interest. Aha – the mystery explained.

'I read,' suggested Miss Richardson.

Unfortunately reading did not count as a hobby with Miss Fowles, especially the *small* books Miss Richardson read about sad middle-aged spinsters familiar with the art world. If she had marched her way through four-inch-thick blockbusters of high romance, it might have counted as a proper hobby. Mum could then have told Miss Fowles with some hope of impressing her that Miss Richardson was an 'avid reader'. Reading slim paperbacks which have won literary awards was just regrettable, like varicose veins – almost a minor handicap.

'What about my music then?'

'That's not a hobby either – sitting there listening to symphonies, that's not going to impress Miss Fowles unless you combine it with something else like knitting or crochet.'

'I can't knit.'

'I know.' It was something I knew Mum would admire about her. As one who can't cook, she glories in the ordinary domestic things others can't do.

Miss Richardson couldn't cook, sew, knit, paint, or make strange objects out of grass (which I suggested).

'But I can speak four languages and play the flute,' said Miss Richardson. 'I am not without accomplishments. I didn't remain single through lack of accomplishments!'

'I know,' said Mum, sadly. 'You were a headmistress.'

Somehow the thought of her having been a headmistress is hard to take on board. To have been a tyrant (for aren't they all?) and now to be so nice! Every time I see her, I wish secretly, that she was my grandmother. But perhaps hers was a different school; maybe she got the girls to dance the Dance of the Veils at assembly and let people make up their own songs?

'What about Patience?'

'I detest cards. It brings out the worst in people.'

So I produced my unwanted Christmas gift from the twins: a two million piece puzzle of York Minster and grounds, and together we started it. I hate puzzles: there is a picture, just one picture, and you have to find it. What's more we have added a few tricks to prevent you from finding it easily. Ha! Ha!

'This could be a punishment for criminals. The more terrible the crime, the more sky,' she said.

We turned over each piece and placed all the sky in one pile and the straight edges together.

Then we invented (well, mostly I did) eight things an elderly person might do in the community — including a whist drive, an outing to Winchester with Derby and Joans, Townswomen's Guild, Women's Institute meeting, Church, lecture by the parson's brother-in-law about his travels in West Africa and so on, all of which (excepting the whist)

Miss Richardson thought she might quite like to go to, then remembered that they didn't exist.

'You're going to be exhausted,' I said.

'I am already. Being cunning is so tiring, don't you find?'

I should have said 'I wouldn't know' but there was no point. It was clear to me that Miss Richardson might not have been a tyrant of a headmistress in all senses, but she certainly had a gift. And that gift was in knowing things about you that were not obvious or had not been told directly to her. I felt sure she knew something secret about me. I'm not sure what. Perhaps it was something I didn't know myself yet.

So I said nothing. After all, we were fellow conspirators now, with the common aim of defeating the Foul One. When we said goodbye to her, she gave me a little kiss on my cheek, like a grandmother would.

We arrived at Aunty Bev's during breakfast. The sweet scent of smoked bacon filled the air and I almost dribbled, though I had eaten raw oats with scabby bits of dried fruit soaked in skimmed milk earlier.

Mr Van Haagen was still hiccupping his way through his tea and toast when the twins left and Aunty Bev sat on the bench next to him and said, 'My sister and I want to do a little experiment with you. We think you should get out more, have a bit more stimulus generally. And exercise. Beginning with swimming today.'

'The Channel?' he asked, smiling faintly.

'No, just swimming for the disabled, locally.'

'How very kind.' He smiled at us briefly as his head spun in our direction.

I was determined to make this swim, maybe his last, who knows, memorable.

Chapter 12

IN THE SWIM

The Leisure Centre is also a favourite place for youth to hang out in; around the pool they can be just as scantily dressed as at the beach. However, it costs money. On the other hand it is money your parents are likely to fork out because swimming sounds so healthy. The fact that swimming is the last thing you'll do is beside the point. In fact I adore swimming and usually do a few lengths even when the main point is See and Be Seen. I even have my Life Saver's badge. There is something about weightlessness that attracts me. I am told that as a nine-month-old baby I swam, under water, to the horror of my parents who had let go of me by mistake. I don't remember that, of course.

Through the long sloping intestines of the Leisure Centre we went, along with a bouncy bloke in a tracksuit with the emblem of the Centre across his muscular chest. It was the rather overdone chest of one who spends his time lifting weights. Actually, I don't know why they do it because all the girls I've ever heard talk about it universally agree that it looks grotesque! Especially that bit where they seem to have breasts.

We halted in the very bowels of the building outside doors marked Men Changing and Women Changing. Mum handed over the rolled towel with Dad's fluorescent trunks to the attendant and disappeared into Women Changing. It puzzles me that a man of my father's advanced years (nearing forty!) should need such a garment. But he does wear them.

The scene inside Women Changing on the morning of the disabled swimming was a shock which I think Mum should have prepared me for. Women of all ages and all shapes were in all stages of nudity. My eye couldn't settle anywhere because so much of the flesh visible had bits missing or was shrivelled or the wrong shape. And it's rude to stare. But you want to stare and stare and stare and then say – how did *that* happen? I didn't though. I'm not a complete jerk, and Mum was just changing efficiently as if this were a normal place. A hairdressers, or the bus stop. Not really a vision of Hell peopled by the unlucky ones.

Oh, *lucky* me. Lucky not to be blind or deaf or mute or limbless or spastic or wracked with pain – oh, lucky me to have endless opportunity for enjoying life!

Only – do I?

* * *

We waited for them by the pool's edge.

Mr Van Haagen and the attendant, Steve, approached slowly down the side.

'Here he is, and we won't need the hoist. I've got him to walk.'

'Oh, he can walk if supported,' Mum said. 'Thank you. I can manage now, thanks.'

I took hold of Mr Van Haagen's other arm but Steve did not move away. There was more of Mr Van Haagen than you would suppose seeing the twisting mass of loose clothes in the wheelchair. He seemed quite solid here in the stupid shorts. His legs especially seemed surprisingly smooth and shapely, seeing how seldom he used them. Graceful even, though not straight. He had once been very, very tall.

The swimming pool had glass walls and through them you could see a great grey mass of water not far away: the actual sea. How strange to splash in chlorine within spitting distance of the sea, only a plate of glass and a long lawn away.

Mr Van Haagen climbed down the metal ladder into the water, which was chest-high at the shallow end. He straightened himself up, but could not let go of his head. Still the spasm in his neck and shoulder gripped him. But his legs drifted him outwards. I put my hand on his bony back, urging him forwards.

'Deeper,' I said. I said this because I know that people who can't stand are better off in deep water

– it's to do with water tension which presses in and holds them up.

Someone came in with a wheelchair and Steve moved away to pump the hoist, shouting before he went, 'Remember, you can't help floating – all bodies float.' Yes, I thought, that's right. But face up or down? I suddenly felt worried about my ability to look after him in water.

Had we let ourselves in for something we couldn't handle? And just to prove to Aunty Bev that we could keep him busy if she took on Miss Richardson?

Mum was there, then, barely able to stand. While treading water, she gasped, 'You go and do some lengths Geraldine. Loosen you up for tonight. I'll look after him.'

I was pleased. For some reason I had thought, being the better swimmer, that I'd have to stick with him the whole time. So I set off. Blind people were bombing down the middle with blackened goggles on. A man who looked like Fungus the Bogeyman was breaststroking down one side. I needed something to distract me from all this. I decided to dedicate each length. The first for Miss Richardson packing her veils and her flute, breaststroke. The second, Fran licking stamps, sidestroke . . .

Then I saw, a few metres away in the shallow end, but deep enough, Mr Van Haagen's head shoot outwards from his body as he thrashed and went down. Mum wasn't looking – she was at least two metres away. He disappeared completely. I wouldn't get there in time. I felt my whole self turn to jelly.

Half a minute later Mr Van Haagen reappeared on the surface. I had no breath left myself. I crawled towards him to assist, but there was no need. I could see that underneath him his limbs were moving in a reasonable sort of breaststroke and the deep end with the diving boards was coming closer. He was swimming! And by this time I was having my work cut out to keep up with him since I didn't dare let my face go underwater and lose sight of him.

A figure was squatting at the poolside at the deep end shouting, 'Attaboy, keep going!' – it was Steve, urging him on.

Of course at the time I had no idea what was happening. How was it possible? Had he made a sudden, miraculous, recovery?

Somewhere between the shallow and deep ends, swimming furiously, I noticed that Mum was struggling to join us in the invented sidestroke that she does.

At the deep end Steve told him to rest on the ledge, but as soon as he did so, he was in difficulty – his neck went into spasm and his head moved. In wrenching his left arm upwards to counteract the movement, he lost his foothold on the ledge and span back down into the water. I didn't hesitate – only an arm's distance from me was the gap of water he was under. I took in a mighty breath, slapped my own face into the water and opened my eyes.

I saw him straightaway, about a metre down and twitching, flailing about. His hair was fluorescent white against the murky grey of the background water, like those fibre optic rods of floating light strands. I grabbed out at it with both hands and quite roughly tugged him up and into my arms. He came up fast like a weightless thing and I turned him round so I could push his chin up.

By the time I surfaced behind him, he was choking in air.

So, though I had never done it before to a living being, I Life Saved him. Just like I had with the dummy at school. It must have been no more than ten seconds before I had Mr Van Haagen floating horizontally on the water, face upwards, as I trod water.

Mum looked as if she'd seen a ghost!

'Geraldine, are you all right?'

'Course, Mum. It wasn't me who was drowning.'

'What happened?' Steve asked me but I couldn't say, especially since I was trying not to drown. The weight of my savee was dragging me down. They warn you about this. There is a horrible paragraph in the book where they advise you to kick away the drowning person and *let* them drown if your own life is being threatened. I remember wondering at the time if anyone had ever done that, and if they could sleep at nights afterwards.

I didn't have to. Mr Van Haagen twisted himself round and swam away, towards the shallow end, turned, swam back, and swam back again, all without resting anywhere.

I had saved a life! I'm sorry to say my first thought was – if only I had a waterproof mobile telephone with me and could phone Fran!

Despite our exhaustion, we still had to take Mr Van Haagen back to Aunty Bev's. We told her about the rescue. She frowned and thought for a while and then came up with an explanation: Mr Van Haagen's nerve pathways from brain to neck are faulty, 'dystonic', but when he is faced with sudden death, the nerves find suitable channels, temporarily, to save his life. Really, someone with his disease ought to spend their lives being threatened by terrible danger – then his central nervous system might behave itself.

'Still – no more swimming, I think,' she said, seeing us out the door.

Chapter 13

WALKING ON THE MOON

We rushed round the remainder of the list. Technically, Mum is only fourteen-twenty-fifths of a worker. She works odd hours at odd times and the government can thus boast of employing lots more people than ever before to care for the elderly. Actually it's a swizz because each one is only a fraction of a worker. So we had a flexible list we could stretch round Mr Van Haagen.

Mum was snappy with the old folk, I must admit, explaining that I had made her late though they could not imagine, and neither could I, how that would have affected her timekeeping. I, of course, kept telling everyone I had just saved a life.

I felt like a wreck though, quite suddenly. And now the competition!

During tea I realised that I could not go anywhere, let alone to the competition, with this hair. I had not even brushed it since swimming and the mirror confirmed that it was standing on end in imitation of a parrot recently run down by an express train. I have various products for this emergency, including a long tube of scented foam which hardens on the hair like cement. I applied this and think now that it must have been responsible for the strange light-headedness that took hold of me shortly afterwards.

Dad never comes to the competitions – he says he can't bear it when I don't win and finds it embarrassing when I do. It was a shame that this was the one evening when he hadn't any work to do, though. I could see Mum too wished she could have stayed at home but Aunty Bev had phoned to say she needed her there tonight. I could see why when we got to the dance school.

She had brought Mr Van Haagen! I hadn't seen Mr Van Haagen wearing a hat before. He looked quite striking, though a little pale.

'I bet you didn't realise,' said Aunty Bev, 'that Mr Van Haagen mustn't ever be left on his own. I usually make arrangements with a neighbour if I go out in the evenings. I didn't this evening, to make a point.'

'Got the point,' said Mum, rather unkindly I thought. I suppose the *point* is that with Miss Richardson also, she would need two helpers in the evenings? I remember Mum once complaining to Bev that she and Dad could never go anywhere without a babysitter for me. How the tables have turned!

'And he doesn't really like it – do you?'

Mr Van Haagen shook his head – or perhaps it was just shaking anyway, and then smiled at something behind me. I looked round. A group of small girls in fantastic black and yellow bee-outfits were whizzing round a larger girl representing a flower – and I thought, this is all quite ordinary to me but it must seem glorious and strange to him!

So maybe it wasn't such a terrible idea. Mr Van Haagen strained towards me and whispered, 'Don't think I'll ever forget.'

They should have known better, really. It could kill him because these competitions are marathons in every sense. For the participants, like me, who often have to dance, all out, five heats in a row, the physical exertion is so extreme it's a wonder I've never burst a blood vessel.

Then for the spectators it is an emotional marathon. They have to sit on hard chairs round the edge of the room under burning hot lights, ready to help with quick changes of outfit – from Ballroom to Latin to Disco and back again. They have to sew damage together again, console, congratulate, save chairs, yell in unison with their school all sitting together, the numbers pinned on the backs of the competitors, as if it were a bullfight not a dance. Then they must fight boredom and nausea because the same music (a disgustingly slimy version of any old music with the right *beat*) is played over and over for each heat, presumably to make it fair. And fair it is not because it is never the best dancers who win, because if it were, it would always be me. Well, not always, but more *often*, anyway.

First, the children of the owners of the dance school always win a prize, then any relatives of the judges, then girls whose outfits have cost over four hundred pounds to buy or make, and then, by about fifth and sixth place, some merit creeps in. Whenever someone tells me a couple won sixth place in a national competition, I think they must be good for this reason.

'Explain to Mr Van Haagen what's going on,' said Aunty Bev, already making a bubble-sculpture out of my hair. I need not have bothered with the mousse. She was scraping it all out painfully.

'They are going to make fireworks of themselves and explode,' he said to me.

I laughed. 'Got it in one,' I said.

Eileen had cleverly reserved seats in such a way that Sunil's supporters would have somewhere to sit, next to us. As yet, these seats were empty. I was just beginning to worry about his timing, when they entered – Sunil and, presumably, his mother.

She was just wearing a tracksuit, like my mother (how I wish middle-aged ladies wouldn't wear them!) and I could almost see my mother thinking, with relief, that she looked just as casual as she did. But actually it takes money to look that beautifully casual, and that is something my mother will never understand. To her a tracksuit is a tracksuit and the cheaper the better.

For instance, take Sunil himself. He was wearing

a plain black all-in-one catsuit with a few sequins on the shoulders, but the material was just right, the cut perfect, the legs dead straight (not flared even slightly) and it fitted him as if it had been made with him in mind, which it hadn't because no mum or aunty makes those things — they are bought. Only his was bought in London somewhere, not locally.

The only slightly odd thing was her sandals. Sandals with a tracksuit?

She sat down next to my dear scruffy little mother and I could just hear her introducing herself as 'Anjana, Sunil's mother.'

I'd never before heard my mother introduce herself that way — as simply Geraldine's mother. Good to know she can do it, though. Many's the time I've been just 'my daughter' and nameless!

They must have found something in common straightaway because they were soon chatting like old friends and I silently willed my mother first to be asking her where she bought her clothes (so that she could rush out and do the same) and secondly to remember all the details to tell me later — about Sunil, if that's what they were talking about. What else could two mums discuss but their talented offspring, at this time and place?

I was done. I turned around. Sunil was standing statue-still and watching me.

Aunty Bev had designed and made my Latin American ballroom dress with a mixture of surgical precision and extravagant flair. Of course my height and colouring had been taken into account – the dress hung from one shoulder only, thus taking my height down a little, and the overall tones, under the livid spots of sequined light, were cold blues and jade to compliment the auburn of my hair and high cheek colour, always pink but bright red when dancing, as Aunty Bev had already explained to me. I can see this if I look in a mirror, but this can be fatal – it makes me shrug.

By Ballroom Dancing standards, the dress was restrained. By the normal standards of evening wear in the civilised world, it was theatrical in the extreme. From one shoulder, it swooped down over the chest to form the glittering underarm archway over an oblong hole in the dress which was designed to expose half the front midriff and half the back. The skirt was knee length at one side and rose to just meet the pantyline at the other, the whole skirt having a sort of lace fringe beneath it, which swirled like whipped cream when I so much as breathed. To help movement, which was the whole *point* after all, the entire garment, barring sequins, had been made out of stretch Lycra and fitted like a second skin. Additionally, there were accessories which had been ordered from a catalogue – the small blue feather boa which clipped on the shoulder, the small net and sequin headdress and the wristlets of ruched taffeta.

Sunil smiled at me. What was he thinking? Just about the dancing, I supposed.

By the time the competition started everyone was well warmed up from practising and everyone's nerves, including my own, were thoroughly frayed. I found myself arguing with Aunty Bev about the feather boa for a ridiculous amount of time, and hoping Sunil couldn't hear us.

Mr Van Haagen seemed to be taking an interest at first and even held his head straight so that he could watch certain couples, but, as you do, he soon lost concentration and became restless and fidgety.

The DJ put on the Cha Cha Cha music, and I had a momentary misgiving about dancing with Sunil at all. But the mothers smiled up at me and I smiled back, so the trance was broken. It isn't my best dance, but Sunil was so good at predicting where I'd be after a spin or hockey-stick, it looked like we'd practised hard and often.

It's very difficult dancing with a virtual stranger. This thought made me miss my footing and trip. Sunil caught me and said, 'Careful!' That's all. Not 'shit!' or 'twit', or 'you nerd', or any of the things partners have said to me in the past at such moments. My heart warmed to him a little despite myself.

After the dance I found I didn't want to speak to him, though. I couldn't think of anything to say, so I went up to Mum (poor Mum) and said, angrily, 'You say I'm irrational – you and Aunty Bev are mad!'

'What do you mean?'

'Bringing *him* here. Mr Van Haagen. He looks like he's going to faint! You just did it to worry me. You just want to spoil everything.' I don't even know why I said this.

'No, darling, you don't understand.'

'I'm tired of hearing that.' And I flounced off, as Fran puts it. Mum frowned at Sunil's mother and Aunty Bev who both frowned back — a whole conspiracy of frowning old women! I felt like bursting into tears. I wanted to go home.

But I couldn't, yet.

Despite this upset we did a creditable Disco number in which Sunil moonwalked, as we call it, (involving seeming to walk forwards while moving backwards) and I stretched my right arm up to support the base of my skull and seemed to lift myself off the floor. This looks more spectacular than it is. A murmur from onlookers. The judges, wrongly, must have thought these everyday happenings and awarded us sixth place for the Disco. Needless to say we also only came second in the Cha Cha Cha too, which was one of the world's great injustices, and the winners, a brother-and-sister team, both had the same surname as the owners of the school, a coincidence I'm sure.

Sunil thanked me formally for the dances, as you have to. He seemed pleased, after all, and said, 'I think we did really well considering how spectacularly little time we've had to practise! Some of these couples do eight hours a day.'

'Yes,' said Aunty Bev, collecting up the bits of feathers and things, 'I reckon *any* prize under the circumstances is *brilliant*.'

Yes, it was brilliant; dancing, prizes, glittering

swishing sequins and boas, all the bright wonderful things, but inside me was a big empty sorrow or longing or something quite new I couldn't have put into words, only I felt as if I was in a dark cold place trying to light a campfire without matches or a torch – desolate.

We were all out in the very windy carpark loading up the dresses and Mr Van Haagen's wheelchair and somehow I found myself alone with Sunil in the inky dark and out of earshot of the others; by his car in which his mother was already hunting in her handbag for keys.

He said, 'There's a fifth form disco at my school tomorrow night. Would you like to come?'

My heart threw open the latch of my chest, jumped out onto the concrete, did a quickstep, lit the bonfire and jumped back before I could say, 'Okay.'

Later I mentally kicked myself for such a terrible, casual reply, so empty of meaning. Walking away (the ground was warm treacle) I panicked and shouted back at him, 'Where shall I meet you?'

'At the school. At eight,' he said.

Now I have to work out which school he's at. I couldn't possibly have *asked* him.

My first date. Just like that. The work of a few seconds, that's all. No fanfares, no angels swooping. Just 'okay'. I said, 'Okay. Okay. Okay.'

Chapter 14

ASKING AND TELLING

I know, he's a rat, he was rude to me, I don't really know him. How am I going to explain this turnabout to Fran? I'll say I was hasty. A person can be wrong. First impressions are sometimes way off! Mine often are. When I first met Fran I thought she was a bozo!

Naturally in the car a few minutes later, squashed between Mr Van Haagen and a pile of dresses, I had to seem to enquire most casually about what info my mum had managed to get about him from his mum.

It went like this: 'Nice lady then, Sunil's mum?'

'Yes. Different. Very nice.'

Silence. Was that it? Was that the last thing she would ever say on the subject this side of the grave? Not if I could help it.

'Different how?' I asked.

'Oh, I don't know. A bit religious.'

Stop. That's it folks. I looked at Mr Van Haagen

in exasperation. He understood my anguish, smiled and said to the front – 'Tell us all you know, Mrs Budd.' She was so surprised at this that she turned around and stared at him. I looked out of the window in case she could read anything on my face, the way she sometimes can.

'It's not that she's religious, really, deeply. It's just that she wants the children to know that they have an alternative to Church of England, if they want it. That's all. Because C of E seems so – what did she say – *drab*.' She turned back to Mr Van Haagen and said very pointedly, 'Drab!'

'Yes – I know what she means,' said Aunty Bev. Mr Van Haagen grunted too: he might be Jewish.

'How nice for them. I wish I had an alternative!' I shouted – yes, I'm afraid I did shout though I didn't mean to.

There are lots of things we don't have, of course, like adequate central heating or a dishwasher, but this doesn't bother me. It does bother me not having our own religion. I hate having to put a dash on a form whenever it asks my religion. I think it is the least they could have done – provided me with a system of belief if only to have something to mock at and rebel against. But they haven't, and it is a dereliction of duty on their part. When I asked Dad why, he just said they didn't want to impose on me anything they couldn't believe in themselves and hoped that I would make up my own mind in due course. What could be more rational? Rational yes. Stuff rational!

'You're Church of England,' said Aunty Bev, quietly.

'That's not a religion,' I said, 'it's just a nasty little habit people think they have. It is sheer drabness!' Now I had the word, I wasn't going to let go of it.

Mr Van Haagen laughed out loud.

But at least that had loosened Mum's tongue and she told us all that Sunil was one of three children (two younger sisters), that his father wanted him to be a doctor and spoilt him terribly, giving him a moped the moment he asked for one. Anjana kicked up a fuss about this but was told not to interfere. Sunil was a stubborn boy and knew what he wanted. At school they teased him about his ballroom dancing but at home his sisters wouldn't dare to — he had told them that dancers are fitter than footballers and that had shut them up.

'He gets his dancing from his mother — she was a folk dancer before she married.' I pictured her then in a sari — gold thread on transparent silk and a million anklets and bracelets catching the light — not a middle-aged woman in a tracksuit but a young girl gliding across a makeshift stage in a clearing to a hushed audience under the stars, sitar music playing. Very romantic. Sunil had that in his genes. The translation of it into ballroom dancing was, if anything, rather dull. Drab almost.

When Aunty had dropped us home, Mum and I scavenged in the kitchen.

'Mum, I'm going out tomorrow night,' I said, offhand as if it was something I did every day.

'With Fran?' she asked.

'Um, no.'

I got out the cheese and crispbread noisily.

'Who then?'

'Soooo –' I muttered.

'What? Speak up.'

'With Sunil.' Her mouth fell open. It really did!

'His school are having a fifth form thingee and I'm going with him. It'll be a dance.' (Somehow I thought calling it a *dance* was a good move: it sounded so old fashioned and ordinary. Also some people call what I do social dance to distinguish it from ballet which you do on your own.)

'Well, you'll have to ask your father.' Actually I realised then that I hadn't been asking. I'd been telling her.

'Why?'

'To drive you there,' she said.

'I can take the bus,' I said, trying to be rational, like they are. Or think they are.

'Miles!' she called. It was that 'come and sort this out' voice.

He came. I let Mum do the explaining. After all, I had no problem. She told him that I wanted to go out to a dance with a boy we hardly knew, *who rode a motorbike*. Then I pointed out, rationally, that she had met and liked his mother at the competition and had herself praised him for being so polite, and I would not be riding on the *scooter*.

101

This seemed to sway Dad, and we reached a compromise, just as Fran is always advising. He would take me and collect me, at a pre-arranged time, but I was allowed to go. After I'd left they were talking softly about something and I'm sure I heard Beverly mentioned.

Thank goodness he didn't ask me *which* school: I would have looked a right fool not knowing.

Fran would know how to find out.

Fran was glad to hear from me, and was meaning to phone me. She had some funny stories to tell about her Wednesday, which had been spent in awful anticipation of tomorrow, big Thursday – Pension Day – and the great dread of it which had been instilled in her by Ethel, the postmistress. Apparently, hundreds of thousands of old ladies make the once weekly trek from their homes to the post office just to tell the cashier their life stories while she cashes their pensions. The trick is to deal with each one calmly and fast, so as to keep their custom, for without it, the post office would get the chop from the top. I listened patiently to all this, bursting to tell her.

Then I told her about Sunil and my first date. She was not over impressed.

'I thought we found him rude and unfriendly.'

'Well, first impressions, you know. I've changed my mind.'

'I thought you might.'

'What do you mean?'

'Oh, never mind. Three days off school and you've got a date! You always land on your feet. How do you do it?'

'It's just my extreme charm and beauty, I guess.'

'Where are you going for this date?'

'That's the trouble, Fran. I don't know.'

'The usual thing is to rendezvous at the cinema showing the movie you are going to see,' she said, in her sarcastic voice.

'No, it's a dance. At his school.'

'Ah!' she laughed. 'He's at the Grammar School, then. My snotty little brother has been skivvying for the Filthy Fifths all week to decorate the hall for the disco.'

There was no resentment in her. I've often wondered why Fran isn't at the girls' Grammar School especially since her brother is at the boys'. She's certainly brainier than any of the teachers who teach her. I've asked her about this, and she just says that it's given to some to go there and not to others. This isn't a good answer, is it? She has also said, and this is even more puzzling to me, that by rights I too ought to be at the Grammar if only I'd pull my finger out. But people from there go on to university, become lawyers and doctors, like Fran ought to. From our school, waitresses emerge fully fledged with sour faces and rougher accents than they entered with.

I don't mind. It doesn't matter what school a ballroom dancer attended. You don't hear 'made her own dress and studied at Oxford' on *Come*

Dancing, do you? But Fran needs a head start – she has no obvious talents. Other than her brain, I mean.

So I heard myself saying into the silence at the other end of the line, 'Do you want to come, Fran?'

I really really really didn't mean to say it! Even as the words sped out of my lips, under their own propulsion, I was hoping, I must have been, that she would refuse.

'Oh, you don't mean it, do you?'

'Sure.'

'But he hasn't invited *me*. How could I?'

'I'm sure he wouldn't mind.' (Well, he might!)

'Okay,' she said. The same word I'd said.

'Good. See you there then. Eight o'clock.'

Dear Diary,
Wednesday has been one of the momentous days of history for me – MY FIRST DATE! Tomorrow at eight. 21 hours to wait. It rhymes! Unfortunately, I have invited Fran, by mistake. I'm not all that horrified:

1. my parents will feel relieved knowing Fran will be there.

2. if I can't think of anything to say, she will and

3. if Sunil really wants to see me on my own, he will have to ask me out again.

Also, boys may come and go but a Best Friend is forever.

Chapter 15

THE MALL

My dad reduces everything to its minimum, so even though it was obvious on Thursday morning that storms were coming (claps of thunder followed by flashes followed by more claps and so on), he insisted on shaving electrically near a half-open window by the tree which is waiting for lightning to strike it.

He also thinks nuclear bombs won't really destroy the planet — they'd probably just make you feel rather unwell for a while.

But I don't care today. It is the day of the *date*. Nothing is going to upset me today.

I got up and brushed my teeth for the first time as a Dated Person. Then I brushed my hair for the first time. It felt different, actually. Quite different.

The phone rang twice, for the first time in the house of a Dated Person . . . Mum came up saying Aunty had rung to say Mr Van Haagen would love to go to the new shopping Mall, didn't we think, and Miss Fowles had rung to say she would visit Miss Richardson that afternoon. I gasped at the second piece of news – partly because I had almost forgotten about Miss Richardson. How could I? Mum said she had offered, as casually as possible, to accompany her and she accepted. If she had not accepted, we would have turned up anyway of course.

'What busy bees you are,' said Dad, overhearing all this. Much as I love my dad, sometimes I find his cheerfulness a teeny bit annoying first thing in the morning.

Of course we had to warn Miss Richardson about the Visit, trying at the same time to calm her. We managed an incredible amount of packing in half an hour largely because she was, deep down, a very well organised person and in control of her possessions, even the ones she seldom saw. Mum once advised me as a rule for happiness that if I ever married and had my own home, never to allow a cardboard box to reside within it for more than a week. Dad said, rather sarcastically I thought, that this would probably be the one piece of advice I took.

Since we had to hurry through the rest of the list, we pacified some of the other clients, as I am now learning to call them, with the promise that we would buy them Ginseng, vitamin B, Sanatogen and Complan at the Mall later.

So it was well before lunch when Mr Van Haagen

and Mum and I set off for the Mall in Aunty Bev's car.

It's strange really that we keep taking Mr Van Haagen to places where teenagers hang out. The Mall is such a place. Supposedly free, but you always end up buying yourself a milkshake somewhere out of boredom. Of course, at this time of day, on an ordinary school day, there was no one there under eighteen, except babies.

Apparently there were no Malls in this country earlier in the century, when Mum was a girl, in the Dim and Distant. America had them. I've heard that at Edmonton Mall in Canada there is a whole Disneyworld type experience in the middle.

This makes sense in a country where twenty foot of snow appears in December and stays for six months, when you die of exposure in the awesome cold if you leave your stalled car. There you need to live and shop indoors for half the year. Here we don't. So that's Enterprise for you – as studied by me in Business Studies. I always worked in groups for this subject. Fran was always in the group. I did nothing – but I do remember being told that ours was an Enterprise Culture (Fran probably told me). So, American companies are building these shopping centres over here at the rate of one a week, because they are doing Enterprise: by bringing us the solution to a problem we haven't got.

Or is it that we now expect our entire population

to be in wheelchairs by the year 2000?

'Science Fiction shopping starts here,' I said to Mr Van Haagen as we entered, the automatic doors whispering us in. It was a direct quote from Fran.

'Got my laser gun!' he replied.

It is like the inside of some huge space module. No sky here. I could do with some sky. I feel trapped immediately. There is smoky glass panelling and hidden lights. No real walls, no outsides, though the dummies in shop windows are frozen in outdoor scenes of ecstasy, tableaux of plastic people in arrested flight through this electric sky.

'Geraldine, slow down! It's not a race. Mr Van Haagen will get dizzy!' My mum was having to trot to keep up with us.

'No, he won't. He loves it. He's got his laser gun.'

'Have you gone mad?' she asked me.

'So long as we all go mad together,' he said, his breath running out.

The light falls in pieces from too much glass and perspex, rods of – could be light or water. Small drips of something scatter upwards through tubes of perspex into the sheer air above – I guess this is a twenty-first century fountain.

Beneath it is a pool of water into which the shoppers have thrown money, presumably having bought everything else, they have not fulfilled their dreams and still wish wishes.

I am wishing – for nine hours to vanish. How awful to wish your life away like that.

108

We started to wander down the aisles of a store so big you can never see the end of an aisle until you are at it. Mum declared me unfit to drive a wheelchair so she pushed Mr Van Haagen and commented on the goods displayed. She does this, annoyingly, whenever we go shopping. Dad and I just want to go through the list, pick out the essentials and leave. Not her. She has to remark that frozen rice must be the silliest invention ever, that jams with reduced sugar must go off fast, that cling film is on offer because it has been found to be dangerous to health. Oh look, she'll say, they've got minced woodcock, minced pork and turkey. And she knows *why* – because minced beef, the staple food of us all, is now suspect. Hence they are selling minced everything else.

A nasty thought – might there be a market for minced Mother?

Several aisles commented on and the final one (socks and stationery and the Ginseng at last) just turned into, when she stops, wheels round and says to me, 'Geraldine, will you stop it!'

'What?' What have I been doing? Shrugging? And if so, how could it bother her, anonymously in a shop. I wasn't even that *near* her.

'Dancing! This is *not* the place.' Even Mr Van Haagen was laughing. I realised then that I had been dancing – a slow waltz down the aisles. Can you blame me? Happiness spilling over.

Actually Sunil and I were being featured in a full length documentary on television about

Great Young Dancers. We had just astonished the world by being the youngest ever couple to win an International Dancethon and the commentator was putting this down to extreme talent . . .

I'm sure no one in the shop minded. No one but Mum, who is embarrassed whenever anything is out of the *normal*, the ordinary, the drab standard thing.

'Sorry,' I said. 'Just a bit bored.'

'Bored!' she shouted. I shouldn't have said that. It is an incendiary device to all parents. Say restless or suicidal or mad, but never bored!

'Then go over there and get all the remedies we promised people and see if you can remember them all. If you leave one out, it'll be your fault.'

Ginseng, Vitamin B, Sanatogen. Oh God – the shelves were bristling with pills to slow ageing, pills to fortify the over forties, to help with female problems, to energise children, even (and this would fascinate Fran) to improve your IQ! There was nothing to make old people appreciative of their Home Help. I took a random selection and placed them in the basket on Mr Van Haagen's lap. He looked briefly down at them, between spasms as it were, as if I had slid a bucket of dead fish into his lap.

'Witchcraft,' he said.

We fought our way through to the till and left the shop. Mr Van Haagen waved his hands about in a sort of sign language to Mum, who said, 'Time for coffee,' and parked him and his wheelchair by a bench behind which was a giant trough of emerald plastic plants.

It was like parking a toddler in a pushchair. As a protest, I stayed with him, sitting down gratefully on the bench. In front of me was a wooden rhinoceros with a slide down through its middle. Children were jumping head first into the animal's mouth and reappearing from its varnished brown buttocks, very much like droppings landing on a black rubber tray.

'This will amuse us no end, won't it?' I said.

'They are sacrificing their children to the bullock,' he said.

I laughed. Mum re-entered the stream of shoppers, dodging about like a small grey bullet in her duffle coat.

Mr Van Haagen was beside himself. Literally. She had parked him at an angle to a television showroom and the spasmodic twisting of his neck insisted that he gaze into it. And there he was, in his wheelchair, shuddering slightly, in his grey felt hat, on a screen. As I watched, he waved his free arm in the air, grabbed his hat and waved it at the wall of glass. Inside the screen mirrored his every movement. An old, old man sent a black trunk into the air and threw his hat in an arc out of the screen. The gesture was like someone throwing off a tie after a long day at work. Mr Van Haagen brought his arm back down. The hat was gone. He had been testing the truth of this moving image. How can a man born before the motor car was invented, understand this?

I retrieved the hat for him. Some children had stopped sliding and stared at him, laughing and crowing.

'What you staring at?' I said, crossly. 'He's a famous person on the television!' That shut them up. It was like my dancing — something out of the ordinary.

'I have just had a happy premonition,' he said, smiling. I put his hat back, tilted, like Humphrey Bogart.

Mum came back disappointed, saying the queues were so long at the coffee place it was like Russia. She's never been to Russia so I suppose she means films she's seen on the television.

We wandered along disconsolately towards the car park and suddenly I spotted an empty ice-cream parlour. Häagen-Daz. Empty!

'I've become an ice-cream!' said Mr Van Haagen.

I whined and pleaded so horribly, Mum had to take us in. It soon became obvious why it was empty. A small dish of ice-cream cost, as she put it, as much as the taxi fare home. Then Mr Van Haagen did a strange thing. He grabbed at Mum's hand and plunged it into the breast pocket of his jacket. It emerged with a five pound note.

'I'd like to treat you,' he said. At first Mum wouldn't have it. Normally she's not mean, although she never has quite enough money, I know, but something about the *absolute* expense of it annoyed her. I don't see anything that way. As absolutes. To me, it's just what things cost and has nothing to do with taxi fares. But then I don't have to earn the money – yet!

In the end, she let me buy us ice-creams, though she wouldn't have one herself, and I think it tasted unusually good – worth all that money. Like Sunil's mother's clothes – quality is something my mum can't appreciate.

While we were eating Mum wrestled with packaging: she managed to snap a fingernail trying to score a slit down one side of the thick cellophane around the glued box around the untearable blister-pack of the sealed Ginseng. The Vitamin B had only thick cellophane around a box around a child-proof bottle which was half full of cotton wool. She even removed the cotton wool. The contents of both packages would have fitted into a large eggcup but on the table beside us was a pile of cellophane and packaging about the size of a football.

'Why should those large airtight yogurt containers also have circular plastic seals around the joint between the lid and the tub?' she asked.

'To prevent terrorists tampering with them,' I put in. But she was well away now. Mr Van Haagen is everyone's ideal captive audience, once you get away from the fact of his never being still, as a good audience should be.

'Why can't all containers be as simple to open as matchboxes, or those clever little plastic squares on bread bags? Why are tablets encased in hard gum then put into blister packs too tough and incomprehensible for elderly people to open, not to mention swallow? Why is packaging so *unfriendly*?'

'Or why do washing machines have windows?' I said, just to confuse things.

Mr Van Haagen laughed. I was getting to like him. I could easily think of several more tedious people to spend an hour with than him. Perhaps one day I could take him somewhere really good, like to a movie?

So I felt egged on.

'Well, no one would ever be wanting to look *out* of it. Could it be for entertainment – to see the clothes spinning? What really is the significance of that porthole?' I frowned meaningfully. Mr Van Haagen laughed. Mum sighed, scooped up the waste and took it to the wire bin which was full of similar rubbish.

'It'll be your future that's trashed,' she muttered as she went.

True. Trucks would come to empty these wire bins, taking the packaging to tips, dumping it, and gradually quarries full of the stuff would overspill onto housing estates, gobbling them up, onto roads, snarling the traffic. And all in the interest of hygiene, so that no dust settles on the Ginseng, itself a sort of Korean dust: Mandrake as the school Shakespeare calls it. No laughing matter, really.

Maybe Aunty Bev was trying to show us

something? I was beginning to think that Mr Van Haagen was also a sweet old thing when you get used to his ways and his odd sayings, though totally different from Miss Richardson. The elderly are much nicer than the middle-aged: they have more daring and at the same time, more dignity. Even his odd way of talking is somehow friendly. In the car, going home, he summed it all up with, 'Reholstering the laser-phaser now, Geraldine.'

Of course, English is not Mr Van Haagen's first language.

Chapter 16

REGROUPING OUR FORCES

After lunch we were supposed to rest. We were supposed to gather our strength for the coming visit by the Foul One to Miss Richardson.

But it didn't work out like that. First Mr Van Haagen would not rest at all. So we sat in Aunty Bev's sitting room, with the radio on.

The suspense seemed to mount. Mum became as fidgetty as Mr Van Haagen and went to help with the washing up. The twins came in and asked, as one, if they could watch *Neighbours* now.

Their way of watching television is interesting: they sit next to each other on Aunty's sofa and spread a cloth over their knees to make one lap. Then, one of them passes strands of raffia from a hessian bag across to the other. Between them they weave, their heads bent down and their little hands bobbing and scratching away furiously. If they see the programme at all, it must be only as a slight reflection over the tops of their glasses. They might as well listen to the radio, Aunty often says. But then, *Neighbours* isn't on the radio, is it?

I turned off the radio and put on the television.

Mr Van Haagen sat there jerking and straining, no more able to watch it than a blind man. He was trying though, I could see that. I had an idea.

I went and stood behind him and cupped my hands round his jaws from behind. At first his head rocketed about, sending out his long white hair like streamers in the wind – I was trying to brace him. This wouldn't work. I was making it worse. Then I loosened my grip and the funny thing is when my hands were barely touching his beard, the jerking came to a halt. It was like homeopathy – the shadow of a shadow of a real thing, but powerful.

'Thank you,' came a gruff grunt from below. He was staring at the television. His beard wasn't rough and prickly as I'd expected – it was silky smooth.

I kept up this magic for ten minutes until Mum came in and said, 'Put this on.' It was a blouse of Aunty's. She had made herself up in that horrible evening way she does for a party (bright blue eyelids, pink lips).

'Why?'

'We must look our best.' Well, she certainly wasn't looking her best! I let go of Mr Van Haagen's head, which objected and began dancing about on his shoulders again. I went into the kitchen and changed. It was a lovely blouse, one with tiny frills and lots of vertical darts. Mum and

Aunty Bev looked at me as if I was an exhibit.

'Slightly less of a scruff,' said Aunty Bev, smiling.

I know they hate the baggy things I wear ('with a figure like yours, why hide it?') but Heaven knows I have to wear enough skintight outfits for dances to satisfy them!

Passing through the sitting room, I was hailed by Mr Van Haagen. No doubt he wanted to thank me again, or explain.

'I have one ambition left,' he said, holding his head as still as he could, 'to die bravely!'

All the way down Southbourne Overcliff I was thinking, how on earth could Mr Van Haagen avoid the coward's death – in his bed? I could understand this ambition. Not to slip unawares in your sleep onto that other plane, but to go gallantly, giving your life willingly for something greater than you, (Truth, Freedom, Liberty) and at that moment of death, being there to greet it.

'Such a romantic,' said Mum, 'as if it matters *how* you die.'

If that's the case, then what are we doing drawing up in front of Miss Richardson's flat at one forty-five on a Thursday afternoon, me in a borrowed blouse, her in her war paint, preparing to do battle with the Foul One?

Chapter 17

THE VISIT

Apparently, procedure is to wait outside the block
for Miss Fowles. She knows that Mum knows that
how she gains entry is crucial. Mum mustn't be
there to let her in or she might blow everything: this
had to be Miss Richardson's solo performance.
With helpers.

Five and a half hours to wait until the Date. I
declared war on my daydreaming — I was going to
concentrate *totally*. Miss Richardson deserved it.

So we waited in the drizzle for sight of Miss Fowles'
BMW pulling up a good nine inches from the curb.
Curb-shy as Dad says. Most people fail their driving
test because they've only a vague idea of the
dimensions of their own car.

She is wearing extraordinarily high heels. Why?
Short I suppose, though it only seems to increase
her stature, her shortness. As if to say it is sheer
extravagance and waste to be any taller than I am.

We all walked together into the block, not talking and waited impatiently at the door to the sound of someone inside in a low wheelchair straining to reach high bolts and pull them open.

'This would be a hell of a break and entry job for the police. I can hear Sergeant Wilson asking if this was wise?' said Miss Fowles. Funny, I can't hear anything.

'You can't be too careful though, can you, nowadays?' Well done, Mum – it's for *security*. I can see Mum is on the ball. We are going to be okay.

The door suddenly swung open and there was Miss Richardson, in black, in her wheelchair.

'Ah, it's . . .' she said, making Miss Fowles introduce herself, putting her at a disadvantage. Good, and getting better.

'Miss Fowles, dear – Chief Organiser, Home Help. Can I come in?'

Miss Richardson smiled over-sweetly, condescendingly, but forgot to ask for any I.D. as Mum had told her to – a mistake I wasn't sure whether Miss Fowles had noted. Mum made an attempt to cover it up: 'Of course, we go back a long way,' she said, meaning, *that* is why she need not ask for ID, but the Foul One said, 'I know that, Mrs Budd,' and to Miss Richardson, 'Sorry to put you to so much trouble.'

'No trouble at all. Most welcome, do come in.' The wording was perfect, almost, somehow, a put-down, but the delivery was no good because she seemed to have exhausted herself unlocking the door and could not find enough breath to give the proper intonation to what she said. Instead a breathy tumble of words fell out of her mouth.

After some pleasantries about the fine weather (was Miss Richardson supposed to contradict her?), the views from her flat (all unavailable to Miss Richardson owing to the height of the wheelchair, a fact overlooked by the award winning architects) and some back-and-forth praise of the Home Help organisation in general and Mum in particular, Miss Richardson offered Miss Fowles a cup of tea.

'Oh no, I don't want to cause any disruption, I only came to see how you were getting on,' — thinking, you couldn't possibly get me a cup of tea.

'Oh, it's no trouble.' Oh yes, she could, and would. She wheeled out, faster than I could have trotted, whizzing perilously close to a wicker magazine rack which wobbled in her wake. It wobbled but did not fall. Her sudden departure left Miss Fowles in a difficulty. She slowly rose and went into the hall towards the toilet. Not because she needed to use it (I'm sure she made sure to go before she came out) but to have a look.

'It is spotless,' she said, 'but I assume that's your work, Isobel, or could indicate that she seldom bathes.'

'She's a meticulously clean lady, I can tell you,' Mum said, trying not to overdo it. Would she dare ask Miss Richardson how often she *bathed*? Oh, I hoped not.

While she scouted in the other direction, in the bedroom, Mum zipped into the kitchen to assist. I kept look out by the arch. Miss Richardson was shamelessly pouring the thermos of tea Mum had made this morning into a teapot.

Then she said, 'Biscuits! Good heavens, how could we have forgotten?'

The biscuits were in the overhead cupboard: malted milk. She took the long handled slice from a drawer, opened the cupboard and hooked out a packet of biscuits from inside. The effort left her breathless. The biscuits fell onto the formica surface, unharmed. Mum was just dithering, nervously. No help at all.

But this packaging is like the chemist's and the manufacturers had so designed the packet that no human being could gain entry. Perhaps their thinking was that the customer would then rush back to the shop and buy another – oh, I can't open this one, I'll have to buy another, and now.

'Never mind. I'll put them on the tray and she can open them.'

'Can I help at all?' It was Miss Fowles at the door beside me. I had been so distracted by the biscuit saga, I'd forgotten to spy. Miss Richardson spun round in her chair.

'No, no. You go back and sit down. Ready in a jiffy.' And she wasn't long at all. Mum sprang back to her chair in the sitting room. How Miss Richardson managed the tray on the wheelchair is beyond me. I shut my eyes at the crucial moment, near the magazine rack.

'Do have a biscuit, Miss Fowles. Help yourself.'

'No, thank you. I'm on a diet. You have one though. Build you up, you look a bit on the slim side.'

Miss Richardson picked them up, defeated. Damn. One to the Foul One.

'Bland taste, malted milk: not my favourite.' Fussy about food, Miss Fowles must be thinking.

'I'll open them,' I said cheerfully. I couldn't bear those biscuits sitting there, like an accusation.

'There's a good girl,' said the Foul One. Oh no. Had I committed an error?

There was a silence. Miss Richardson spilt some tea down her front and did not react, even though it must have burnt the top of her chest. She must have been thinking that if she didn't react, Miss Fowles wouldn't notice but I know that Miss Fowles would be registering a problem with personal hygiene.

Then she said it, 'How often do you manage a bath, dear?' She actually *said* it!

'I beg your pardon?' The full headmistress eyebrows!

Miss Fowles realised she had gone too far, and retracted.

'I notice you don't have a shower; I prefer a shower myself, don't you?'

'Yes,' said Miss Richardson, fast, 'I have heard they are more economical. In fact, I'm surprised they don't use them more in Council Housing. It's not a worry with me. I'm afraid I simply fill the tub and luxuriate; bother the expense, you only live once.'

'Yes, true.' Brilliant. I dared to sip my tea. We were winning again.

Feeling, I suppose, she was winning, Miss Richardson launched herself into a speech. 'Those delightful shoes of yours remind me of something. I had a girl once in one of my classes, an eleven year old, who called stiletto heeled shoes 'Biggles' and I couldn't think why. Then I heard one of my younger teachers walking briskly down the hall on the parquet flooring. Her feet went *biggle-biggle-biggle-* so I thought that's it, it's onomatopoeic. When I saw her mother next I told her, but she said, "No, it's not that, it's from 'big heels' which she couldn't say as a baby." Things are not always what they seem.'

Miss Fowles stared at her as if she hadn't understood a word of this perfectly good story.

'And Geraldine here wears them for ballroom dancing, though what could be more unsuitable, I don't know,' added Miss Richardson, as though that were the punchline.

Miss Fowles looked at me and then at the puzzle on the table before us. 'I see you have taken up jigsaw puzzles.'

'Yes, this one is York Minster. As it was, of course, before the fire. I hear they've rebuilt the North transept now, complete with new bosses.'

Suddenly I noticed a treacherous film of dust on the pieces, proving our falseness.

'Bosses? Do you mean under new management?' If she'd ever watched *Blue Peter*, as I do, she'd have known what 'bosses' were.

'They said,' Miss Richardson continued, concentrating hard now, 'that God was showing his displeasure with the bolt of lightning, the Bishop of Durham and all that; but I think He provided a few hundred stonemasons and carpenters with marvellous work for four years, deliberately. After all people are more important to Him than buildings, aren't they?'

Miss Fowles looked blank.

'I think God is worried about unemployment, you see,' Miss Richardson said. Oh, I wish she hadn't, the conversation was becoming more and more weird by the minute.

'Do you manage to get out to church on Sundays?' Miss Fowles asked, pursuing her own enquiries no matter what. Though now I think of it, she might have been following up the religious theme.

'Well, yes usually,' she lied.

'Which church is that, then?' We hadn't decided this. I panicked. Mum and I knew no churches nearby, or anywhere. Well, that's not true, I knew of St Paul's in London but that's no help.

'All Saints.'

Oh, brilliant – there was bound to be one somewhere in town called that. But Miss Fowles knew churches, and we should have guessed this.

'That's a long way to go, isn't it?'

'Yes, but my friend prefers it. She knows the vicar.'

One lie will lead to another and before long . . . how often must Miss Richardson herself have warned her pupils of this? To hide her embarrassment, she adjusted the chair slightly, as if to get the sun out of her eyes, though there was no sunshine today. In wheeling a few inches backward she upset the rickety table with her foot and half the pieces swirled off onto the floor. Naturally she couldn't pick them up now since it would involve incredible manoeuvring, and Mum and I were frozen to our chairs, not daring to help. So instead, she turned the chair around and inched the table towards the wall.

'Silly me. I'm always doing that,' she said. *Why* did she say that?

'You get used to things eventually,' said Miss Fowles, behind her, rather absently.

Miss Fowles, with hideous accuracy, had managed to gaze into the appointment diary by the telephone.

'Ah, you've discovered my secret,' said Miss Richardson, conspiratorially.

'Yes,' said Miss Fowles, slowly. 'Which secret might that be?'

'That I am quite the social butterfly!'

'Yes,' said Miss Fowles, picking up the diary and openly staring at it. 'You certainly are. In fact you ought to be at a meeting right now.' She looked her in the eye. I could have screamed.

126

'Ah, that's been cancelled.'

'Has it? Then it's a wonder you didn't cross it off in your diary.'

Now it seemed to be open hostility. The weapons were out in the open, the swords drawn. Miss Fowles wouldn't call her a liar, or anything so crass, but she had won, and Miss Richardson shrank physically into her chair.

Miss Fowles put the diary down and, moving towards the window, spoke.

'You can't leave the flat, can you? You're trapped here, dangerously alone, even going to the toilet must be a trial. People seldom call, except the girls I send you and the milkman and the social worker once a quarter, if that. You manage from day to day, being careful not to fall or give any trouble to anyone. But you are not forgotten, and I don't intend you to end your days on the floor of some rented room with a broken hip, pain shooting through your body, unable to call for help. I know where my duty lies, and it is a false and stupid sentimentality to say you are better off on your own – in a house without adequate nursing care. Buildings are just buildings, and like God, I think people are more important than buildings. In a nursing home you would be looked after, fed, kept warm, have company, go on outings, be able to pursue real hobbies for the disabled, you might even make friends. Anywhere else, you are only waiting to die.'

I opened my eyes and saw that Miss Richardson

was crying rivers.

Miss Fowles, her duty over, left swiftly, her biggles making no noise on the carpeted stairs.

Chapter 18

THE ROW

We were left in that dark room with a sorrowful Miss Richardson and I remember making her all sorts of promises but I can't remember what. We were unable to comfort her much. Mum kept repeating that she wouldn't let it happen, that there was a dining room at her sister's.

Talk of sisters and dining rooms did not seem to make any difference. She kept wailing that she had been condemned like an old, unsafe building, that she had been *condemned*.

Finally we left and went and sat in the car. Neither of us spoke because there was nothing to say. All the words in the world had been used up. The Foul One had gathered up all the good ones, twisted them till they screamed in agony, and spat them out. There were none left breathing.

My mind felt empty and there was a sour taste in my mouth.

'Let's go home,' I said.

We made our way home silently. *Miles Better Motoring* was parked outside the house, thoughtfully on the street so that Mum could use the driveway.

'Dad's home early,' she said.

Mum hardly said hello. Poor Dad. She just began shouting in the middle of the kitchen, shaking.

Miss Fowles had really done it this time. The woman was a monster. She regarded people as little more than numbers to shuffle round on her designer clipboard. She spent more on her shoes than most elderly people could spend on food in a week. She was no judge of character – everyone was, to her, the same. Senile. Stupid. Didn't know what was good for them. People like Miss Fowles ought to be locked away, not given power over others.

Why hadn't she said all this at the time?

'Yes, but she's in charge. You'll have to go by what she says,' said Dad, quietly.

'Where's your compassion? I'll have to resign. I can't just go along with cruelty.'

'No, you can't. You can't ever let anyone down; it is a great weakness. If you disappointed someone they would think badly of you and you couldn't bear that. A person without enemies: that's you.'

Honestly, I saw no need for this *personal* attack at all. It was simply a dilemma to be solved like in Religious Ed. What had the, possibly true, facts about her personality to do with it? On the other hand, I think we need her money from this job: I am not quite ready to go out to work myself yet!

They argued, and then they shouted, and then it became a fully fledged row. First Mum said she shouldn't have bothered to discuss it with him; call this a discussion, he said; everything's personal with you, she said; where's your flexibility, he said; where's yours, she said, and so on.

I left. I was not needed there. They could row perfectly well without me. Better, in fact: knowing that I hate rows almost more than anything (well, except perhaps nuclear war), they might feel they had to tone it down.

Also, it was time to have four baths, wash my hair twice, and choose what to wear eleven times. I knew I would dither, so I had better get started now. All this other stuff – Miss Richardson, Mr Van Haagen, jobs – was all just nonsense on the edge of my life. At the very centre, the core itself, stood Sunil, waiting for me by the school gates. He would not be there yet, I knew that. But all day I'd been imagining him there.

And Fran.

Oh God, Fran! While washing my hair I decided I'd have to somehow dissuade Fran from coming. How? Tell her it's all off? I'm sick? She wouldn't believe that. I didn't really want to lie to her. Perhaps I could just tell her the truth – that I didn't really want her there.

And then on Monday, and the rest of my life?

'Hello, Fran. It's Geraldine.'

'I know. What is it? What should you wear, say, think? Where shall we meet?'

'No, I just, er, feel rather worried.'

'Oh, cold feet. Quite natural.'

'No, it's not that.'

'What then?'

'I don't know. It's just . . .' I panicked. How could I say it? 'My paretns are rowing again.' Why did I say that?

'Well, I'm sure that's a good sign. People who don't care for each other are silent. They're just having a Down as in Ups and Downs, I expect. It's not about you, is it?'

'No.'

'It'll be about the Other Thing, then.'

'What do you mean?'

'Put it this way – I know *my* parents don't have sex anymore.'

'Everyone thinks that, but how else could you have existed?'

'No, I know.'

'Why?'

'My dad lives in Norway.' I laughed. But I got the point: at least I have two parents.

You can't ever get the better of Fran – that's one of the many things I like about her. She is always one hundred per cent *right*.

One of the other things is the way she slips in vital bits of info (like her Dad not living with them, which I'd suspected for a long time now) while telling a joke, casually, as if it didn't really matter.

So I decided her presence at the disco didn't matter (to me) either, and I just said where I'd meet her and beautified myself at great length (never was anyone so polished and perfumed as I – I smelt like the cosmetics section of a chemist's). While I did so, I could hear them waging their war. Like all wars, all the ones I have seen on television, it had its furious highs, its lulls, its silences and its crescendos.

The crucial thing is – will Dad still be able to drive me to the Grammar School in time? I walked quietly down the stairs both to look at myself in our only full-length mirror and to listen in to judge whether or not either of them would be giving me a lift to the disco.

Only *fairly* stunning. The trouble is my legs have grown first. Apparently when I was a baby I never crawled because of this: my 'back legs' as Dad called them were so long, my bottom was always much higher than my shoulders and I fell forwards. And now in certain outfits (say, the awful short pleated skirt we *have* to wear for hockey) my legs seem to sprout out of my chin. Fran says, helpfully, that one day I'll grow into my legs. For now, I have to wear knee-length skirts to counteract the legginess and comfort myself with the knowledge that it's this exaggerated amount of leg which makes me a good dancer.

* * *

The row had reached that all-embracing stage where they were seeing each other's opinion on this question in global terms:

'I suppose then there is no such thing as right and wrong?' said Mum.

'Everything is open to interpretation. You always exaggerate so!'

I was going to walk down the hall to the kitchen to ask for a ride, when I heard:

'Beverely warned me about you! I should have known. If you could ditch her, you're capable of anything!'

Dad's reply was too low to hear from this distance, but I didn't need it. I ran back upstairs. I didn't want him to know I'd heard *that*.

I sat on my bed, and burst into tears. Dad ditched Aunty Bev. How could that be? It must have been a long, long time ago. And Aunty Bev is still single and childless. Did he ruin her life? I tried to think of one thing Aunty Bev had said to me on the subject of Dad, and the strange thing is, I couldn't think of a single thing. She had never said even one, slightly sarcastic thing. The restraint! If it had been me, I would have posioned me against him.

Dad came into my room. He never knocks, like Mum does. 'Time to go,' he said, staring at my giant poster of Madonna. He was twirling the car keys round and round in his hand.

As we went out to his car, the air was full of

electricity as if some dreadful storm were on its way. Winds were playing noisily with the roof tiles. The outside world was on the verge, revving up into a rage.

Chapter 19

THE DISCO

Dad once told me the secret of driving defensively. Imagine, he said, that every other driver of every other vehicle is drunk, has just rowed with the wife/ husband, killed them, stuffed their body into the boot of the car, and is now travelling as fast as possible either towards somewhere secret to bury the body or instant suicide, whichever is the sooner. If you think like this, he said, you'll never have an accident. Since I don't drive myself, the effect this has had on me is that in the car with him at the wheel I feel totally safe.

Usually.

Today was different. Obviously, he wasn't drunk. I don't think my father would go so far as to start the ignition after a low-alcohol beer, even if you were pointing a gun at his head. When Mum suggests bringing back hanging for child molesters, he always adds 'and drunk drivers'. But all the evidence of a mind made crazy, of someone in the middle of a row, was here.

He was driving too fast. He had it in for the gear stick. He even punched the heater and said 'shit' under his breath. This is a word I know they have agreed not to use in front of me. He kept overtaking all those other drunk murderers using the same road as him (how dare they) and we made it to the Grammar School, a twenty minute drive, in under ten minutes. Presumably, he was anxious to continue the 'discussion' with Mum. We had not spoken at all.

When we stopped by the main gates, he wiped his face off – a funny gesture where he runs his flat hand down from his forehead to his chin, as if to clear his features and start again – and said, 'What do you think, Geraldine?'

'If you must know, I agree with Mum.' Not because I did agree with her particularly but because he was now cast in my mind as ruiner of Aunty Bev's life, and an unsafe driver who had put my very existence at risk. A thoroughly nasty person.

'You've got to take the long term view,' I told him. Then I got out of the car without kissing him goodbye and trotted off.

I was determined not to let this upset spoil anything. Far more important things were going on, or would be shortly.

Inside the building was a sort of wide hall with pillars and sets of double doors. People were standing around obviously waiting for each other with that vacant I'm-not-really-waiting-for-anyone look. I have practised this very face myself in front of a mirror. I suddenly realised my face must be tearstained. And there was *nothing* I could do about it – it was too late.

There he was. He was beautiful. Why hadn't I noticed this breathtaking fact before?

And there was Fran too. The funny thing was she was standing almost next to Sunil. Of course, since they didn't know each other, they weren't talking. I felt sorry for Sunil, because Fran would know he was *him*, because of his skin if nothing else, whereas there was no way he could have known she was anything to do with me.

Clever, considerate Fran, to stand next to him so that I wouldn't have to choose whom to approach first. I could greet them together.

'I hope you don't mind, Sunil, I invited a friend. This is Fran.' If it had been a test I'd devised, like knights of old had to go through, to test their mettle, whatever that is, Sunil passed with flying colours. He smiled very broadly and said, 'Most guys here are fortunate to escort *one* girl to the dance, and I have the pleasure of two!'

'How courtly of you,' said Fran, obviously thinking along the same lines as me – about the knights. 'I promise not to let you both down. For example, by trying to dance.'

I must say I thought Fran could have made a bit more effort to dress up. The culottes were okay (beige and they fitted her) but the pink top, for it was simply a shapeless woollen garment you couldn't name, just hung most horribly from her thin shoulders, and worst of all, she was wearing her school shoes! I suppose people with glasses have to wear them all the time? Hers weren't even nice ones. Still, I mustn't criticise because some friends of mine might have worn wondrous togs to compete with me and that would have upset me even more. Fran doesn't do herself justice, is what Aunty Bev would say. Even her walnut coloured hair just lay down like a dead animal all over her head.

Sunil was wearing black jeans and a loose T-shirt with *J'adore la danse* printed on it. I had not seen him in normal clothes before, and was impressed. No doubt, if I'd been Fran, I'd have made a good joke out of this – you look different in clothes, or something . . .

The disco was happening in the assembly hall, decked out for the occasion with streamers and balloons.

'The contents of my little brother's lungs are up there,' said Fran as we entered, pointing to the balloons.

'Keeping an eye on you,' said Sunil. They both laughed. I could see they shared the same weird sense of humour.

The room was full of noise. It was noise, *not* music. There is a certain kind of popular music they play at discos which is impossible to dance properly to because of its rhythm. I hate it. It's the one thing

I have in common with my parents, other than living at the same address, that we all hate this type of music. What I hate is that you can't hear any lyrics (what is it *about*?) and the rhythm (one – one – one) is impossible to dance to. My feet say 'you must be joking', curl up and go to sleep.

Fortunately Sunil felt the same way. He looked at me (over Fran's head) and grimaced.

That was when our eyes met. He moved towards me, behind Fran, and said, 'Been crying?'

'No,' I lied. He smiled. Either he believed me or he didn't care. I just let him move away, towards Fran.

We got drinks (non-alcoholic cider) and handfuls of crisps and sat down as far away from the noise as we could. We sat in such a way that Fran was between us. She made a big thing of trying to move so that she wasn't, but it didn't work. I wasn't sure whether I minded.

I couldn't let Fran do all the talking, though. I didn't want Sunil to think I was some kind of a dummy. So, I said the first thing which came into my head, which was about my parents rowing. Obviously I did really want him to know why I'd been crying, though I can't think *why*. I regretted it instantly, but Fran made light of it by saying, 'Having only a single parent, I have to do all the rowing myself. It's really hard work too.'

'My parents never row when we're awake.'

'Considerate of them,' said Fran.

'No. It means my sisters take it in turns to stay

up till midnight to prevent it.' We all laughed. He did a good imitation of a small girl rubbing her eyes, but determined to stay awake.

'Do people listen to this sort of music by choice?' asked Fran.

'I wouldn't,' I said. 'I hate it.'

'I have heard that it's bearable if you're on drugs when listening,' said Sunil.

'I've got my atomiser,' said Fran, 'we could all have a whiff.'

And so it went on. Sunil and Fran got on well. There was never a gap in the conversation for me to say my piece, though what I would have said, I don't know. Afterwards I'll think of dozens of clever things I could have said. I kept thinking that Fran was the brain and I was the brawn, as the saying goes. Together we make a good whole person.

Gradually, all over the hall boys and girls were getting up the courage to dance. They call it dancing. I call it standing nearish to each other and swaying more or less rhythmically and occasionally, at random, moving a limb outwards.

Fran leapt up and said, 'That DJ must have something else.'

She elbowed her way down the hall and went to speak to him. I was impressed. I wouldn't have dared do that!

When she returned, she said, 'I've just requested a jive, and you're going to show me how it's done! I've only ever seen it on telly.'

I felt a panic in me. On the one hand this was what I'd come for – to dance with Sunil without the pressure of Eileen, for *fun*. On the other hand, could it be done without jazz shoes or outfits, or a proper dance floor or a knowledgeable audience? And was I really in the mood now? Would it work?

Sunil was smiling rather vacantly: it was impossible to tell what he was thinking. The record changed. It was the first two bars of *Chattanooga Choo Choo*! An old song but a goodie. I found my feet had woken up, kicked off my shoes and were shouting 'let's go for it!'

There was a space large enough where the dancers had died out, at the food end. Sunil and I were standing facing each other. This space was ours.

Silently, we counted ourselves in. Step-step, quick-quick-miss. Then his arms darted forwards and he flung me with force into a flamboyant spin beneath his arm and counter-thrust me back again. It was a flying start. He never let go of my hand, a frenzied strength propelling each flourish. Then the playing with time which we had rehearsed at the competition to look accidental. In a flash – I rose to fall, before slithering down between his legs, sliding on my bare heels. Twisting round he seemed to punch the air in a salute and I flew up towards it like a fish reeled in. Three times repeated with a twist at the end as the music stopped.

Then I saw that the whole room had come to a halt and the entire population of the assembly hall stood watching us. I shrugged and blushed. There was clapping! But Sunil bowed very low and laughed.

'Wow!' said Fran, 'so that's what you do. I take back everything derogatory I've ever said about your dancing.'

Then a nasty thought struck me. Sunil had invited me here to this disco not because of *me* but because of my dancing. Boys who do Social Dance often have the problem that their male friends, not really understanding it, think them sissy and effeminate for wearing sequins and for doing it. Now he had proved to them for all time what it meant – that nothing could be less effeminate than having a girl in your arms like this for fifteen minutes!

This nasty thought was so strong in me that it welled up and exploded out of my lips.

'Show off!' I yelled at him. I saw Fran step back and tremble. He stared at me.

'What do you *mean*?' he asked.

'Now you won't get any more stick from your mates about your dancing, will you? Now I've done that for you, I'll go, shall I?' I would have too.

'Sorry.' He came and put an arm on my shoulder and gently pushed me towards the table where a pale and trembling Fran was staring at an empty polystyrene cup as if it were a fascinating novel.

'Sorry, sorry, sorry,' he said. 'It's true. I did use you. Or rather, your *dancing*. But you'll forgive me, won't you?' He touched my nose with a forefinger.

Fran said, flatly and without looking up from her

cup, 'Please forgive him.'

It's not easy to forgive someone, even when they're so sorry, but I had every reason to try. If I did leave, for instance, I'd have to walk home, and also, sooner or later I'd be dancing with him again.

So I did. I couldn't help myself – it wasn't really at all difficult. For one thing, he is so beautiful and was being so sweet, I couldn't be cross with him for long. Also he kept telling me, via Fran, how he had misjudged me because I was so quiet, I seemed stupid. Yes, Fran agreed, all her teachers think that too. But now he knew otherwise. We laughed.

Then I felt as if my life was beginning, as if nothing would ever go wrong again. At the next suitable music, we all got up and Sunil and I taught Fran the basics of several modern dances and laughed so hard I thought we'd get hysterical. The music seemed to have improved – the DJ abandoned tuneless, rhythmless disco music and played oldies. The lights went down. I felt intoxicated by movement and by Sunil's energy.

Suddenly it was half past ten and the ordinary lights went on. An ancient man in a tweed suit stood on the stage at the far end and thanked everyone for making this possible and announced that rather a lot of parents were waiting in the car park at the front. Would we collect our coats in an orderly fashion?

There was a great scrum by the front doors and Fran's mother grabbed my collar! 'Oh, hello,' I said.

'What are you doing here?' asked Fran, rather

rudely I thought, given that it was her own mother and she had come out in foul weather and I knew that their car was ancient and seldom worked.

My father had phoned her and asked her to collect us. Presumably this meant he felt unable, due to his anger, to drive safely. Sunil was hanging about looking embarrassed. Fran offered him a lift but he refused.

'I've got a scooter,' he said. Then he brushed his lips against my cheek (a shock passed through me) and disappeared. I felt as if the bottom of the world had fallen away. He had gone, without making any further arrangement to meet.

Fran's mum drove me home, I thanked her and she just said, 'I hope you haven't overdone things. Fran's asthma is bad at the moment. And she has to work tomorrow.'

'Oh, don't fuss, Mum,' said Fran, who did look a little pale, I must admit.

As the car drove off Fran made the 'good one' sign with her thumbs through the car window, meaning she approved of Sunil.

The house was dark and deserted on the ground floor. I suppose I should have been pleased that they hadn't waited up for me, but it was only eleven o'clock and they'd gone to bed! Grumpily I grumped up the stairs.

I knocked and opened their door. A disgusting sight they were: all snugly and lovey-dovey, sitting

145

up in bed with cups of tea and the portable black and white television on.

At their age! I don't know what's worse really — the rows, or the making up afterwards. I almost prefer them raging.

'Had a good time?' asked Mum.

'Yes, thanks. Triffic.' I left them to it. They looked old and sleepy and horribly affectionate in a soggy sort of way. I wondered what had been decided, if anything, about anything. I didn't dare ask — I might ignite the whole thing again.

Chapter 20

WAYS OF GETTING TO SLEEP

Obviously my head was spinning then. No chance of sleep. I lay on the bed trying to still my thoughts. Could not. In my mind danced pictures.

First, Aunty Bev, younger and jiving with a younger version of my dad. Then Mum and Dad shouting insults at each other and kissing alternately in a bowing, ceremonial sort of dance. Then Sunil vanishing and spinning on one leg into a crowd, his almost-kiss burning on my cheek. Then, murky and on the outer edges, Miss Richardson in her wheelchair, veils floating from her head, out of control on a long slope down to the sea where Mr Van Haagan sat twitching and writhing and laughing and eating ice-cream.

No one thing in my life was simple any more.

I picked up the phone. I know you aren't supposed to phone boys. Even Fran would frown on it. But I did. There aren't many people with his surname in our town, and only one lived in his road.

A musical little voice answered: a young girl's.

I'm sorry to phone so late, but could I speak to Sunil?'

'Yes, surely. Is it Geraldine?' My heart leapt up then. His sister knew of me. So there weren't a whole crowd of girls milling around in his life.

'Hello, it's me, Geraldine.'

'Hello, are you at home?'

'Yes, I just thought I'd phone to say, well, to say what about coming to my house after school to practise the Samba?' It sounded so odd, so contrived, so weird.

'Yes, fine. I have a half holiday tomorrow, so I'll come earlier. At lunch time. Okay?' I was surprised at how readily he took it up, but there was something odd and clipped about his voice. I only just remembered to give him the address at the last minute.

It had been a short call. Terse. Afterwards I realised that the phone was in some common room where the whole family might well be watching television, staying up to prevent the parents rowing.

What had I done? No parental permission, I didn't even know for sure that I'd be free — there might be twenty Long Term Elderly to see at three o'clock for all I knew!

Dear Diary,
Thursday night — only one more day of Work Exp

*to go. I think I'm in love, I certainly can't sleep and
may never do so again. My feet are throbbing with
pain. Which reminds me of the electric footspa in
the understairs cupboard which Dad gave Mum. As
yet unused.*

I know I should have gone to bed, but the footspa
was lovely. Very quiet considering the vibration
there is under the one inch of water (two glassfuls
carried quietly from the bathroom). However, far
from making me sleepy, I found it rather
invigorating. I hid it under my bed when I'd
finished, as if it were some rude book I'd stolen
from their bedroom. Actually, there's nothing
naughty about it, lots of dancers use them to
revitalise the feet. Only not in the middle of the
night.

I felt no nearer sleep.

I turned out the lamp, asked myself about the
square root of minus one, and then had the idea of
reading something really boring.

Fortunately the pamphlet on *Home Care in
Dorset* was to hand. I found it fascinating.
Obviously written by Miss Fowles to justify her
existence to the world. Also it was full of lies. I got
up to find a red pen. I would underline all the lies
and post it back to her.

Then I remembered I was trying to get to sleep.

Chapter 21

STEPTOES

I must have slept because I woke up. Unless I just *think* I woke up.

Friday, the last day of my slavery dawned grey and blustery. The word blustery is one I've heard weathermen use and it is a euphemism for hurricane. Radio Solent warned people to stay indoors unless absolutely necessary because of the blustery conditions so I told this to Mum and she said our work was life or death to the elderly, so we had to go.

Finally everything was hitting me. I was in a daze. I failed to brush my teeth, comb my hair, anything.

'What I want from you today,' said Mum, looking disgustingly bright and breezy for someone of her advanced age, 'is a little bit more concentration and a little bit less daydreaming. Is that too much to ask?'

'I don't know. It might be,' I said, 'I don't feel very well.'

'You don't look very well either. And what were you doing with my footspa in the night?'

Talk about illogical – see Fran, where I get it from – I've been brought up *without* logic.

'What's that got to do with daydreaming?'

'I don't know. That's what I'm asking *you*.

'I was just massaging my feet.'

'In the night?'

Fortunately the phone rang then. It was Miss Fowles saying that she had written her letter to the Social Worker and found a provisional vacancy in Pine Haven for Miss Richardson. Fortunately, someone had died. Fortunately for whom? When the place was confirmed, later today, she would ring again and we could do the transfer. Though I could see that Mum had no intention of doing any such thing (she crossed her fingers behind her back so the telephone couldn't 'see'), she said "yes" flatly and hung up. Mum grew in my admiration, despite our disagreement, about four points on a one to ten scale. By the end of the day she might well have the opportunity to score even more highly.

'I'm sorry about the footspa. I couldn't sleep. I thought it might relax me,' I said.

'Yes. You're an odd sort of girl sometimes, Geraldine. That's all.'

'I know,' I said, 'but so lovable all the same.'

She hugged me then, saying, 'Today's the day. By the end of today it will all be resolved one way or another.'

She's the odd one – nothing seems definite to *me*;

unless there's something I don't know.

'You think Aunty will take her, then?'

'Yes. I hope so.'

The weather was ridiculous. Outside the front door, between the porch and the car, the hurricane had concentrated itself into a tunnel. How my mother made the journey, I'll never know, except that being so short and stubby I guess she just presents no edge wide enough for the wind to catch. I, on the other hand, am a totally different shape and present a kind of elongated sail to the wind. I stepped out after her and ended up five metres away down towards the back garden. I must have screamed. Someone did. I could hear Mum shouting, 'Geraldine, hurry up!' — totally unsympathetic to my plight. I had to crawl on all fours *under* the wind to get to the car, and she just got in after me (my door being still permanently shut) muttering something about how silly not to make allowances for a bit of a gust. Bit of a gust! If she calls it that, Dad will have to call it a draught, to show how she exaggerates.

Miss Richardson commented on the dungarees and said I looked like I meant business. I noticed she had no quips or jokes for me now. She was quiet and serious, as if the time for jokes was gone.

Mum wrote down our address and phone number for her 'just in case things go wrong but they won't'. I felt like a soldier just before the battle really gets going — *on alert* as it were. Willing I was, oh so willing, but I didn't like to point out to Mum that she had perhaps omitted to supply me with actual maps or battle plans. She might well have told me all the details when I wasn't concentrating – it's possible.

Miss Richardson was all but packed and had made a little pile of reading matter for herself, as if she had a long journey to go on.

'What's this for?' Mum asked.

'Waiting. Today is the big wait and I need distraction.' She put up her loose arms towards Mum and as she bent down with the timesheet, she gave her a big kiss on the face.

'Hey, you won't do anything silly, will you?' Mum said. It did seem almost a goodbye gesture.

'Do I ever?' she said, smiling. Then I got a kiss too and the heavy powder on her soft cheek must have got in my eyes because they started to water.

'Don't you cry,' said Miss Richardson, 'it's contagious.'

Actually, by the time we left her flat I was sobbing to myself. Suppose it all goes wrong and I never see her again?

Then we had to plough through all the others on the list carefully, leaving nothing out, distributing vitamins on the house. Everyone was pleased with me, even Mrs Stokes who had persuaded someone to prescribe her hormone replacement – at her age! It did seem that my random assortment of herbal remedies were the right ones. I don't think anyone realised I was a temporary thing in their lives – they had just got used to me by now.

Aunty Bev had made my favourite meal for this last lunch – vegetarian lasagna with spinach and tomatoes, real grated parmesan and lemon sludge for pudding. She and Mum seemed to have a plan.

'What's next?' I asked, after lunch, almost dreading to hear what awful thing we would be required to do now. Take Mr Van Haagen dry skiing at Matchams, hang-gliding off Hengisbury Head, free-fall parachuting from Hurn Airport? As a matter of fact, her next instruction cheered me because it hinted that she was making preparations for Miss Richardson.

'Steptoes,' said Aunty. 'I need a bedbase, chest of drawers, and a wardrobe, cheap.'

Well, Steptoes was certainly *cheap* – that was its only nice characteristic. Otherwise it was a dreadful, smelly, huge warehouse of a place where dead people's house contents were thrown higgledy-piggledy waiting for someone to make them an offer. You had to climb over rotting cushions and wrenched off refrigerator doors to find anything and when you did, it was up to you to carry it out of the shop and home. I always thought Steptoes ought to pay their customers for disposing of the goods rather than the other way round.

Anyone could see that to take Mr Van Haagen there would be a disaster of the first order. You wouldn't even be able to get a wheelchair around the place.

Anyone but Aunty and Mum, that is, because we took him! Aunty just said that Mr Van Haagen was enjoying our little outings so much, she wanted us to take him. And besides, she had 'things to do'. Mum didn't dare object.

At Steptoes they were quite nice about it really, and a fat man in a grey boiler suit actually cleared a path through the bedbases for us. But we could only find one chest of drawers which Mum thought suitable.

At first Mr Van Haagen just kept quiet and then he said, to me, 'What does it mean? Why does Miss Walsh require drawers?'

'Um,' I said.

'She's taking in another paying guest,' said Mum.

'But I'm not dead yet,' he said. Mum was obviously shocked by this. Her mouth fell open.

'That's not the point. She'll use the dining room.'

'No she won't. It's her grotto,' he said.

'What's a grotto?' I asked Mum.

'A holy place,' she said, frowning.

She arranged for the chest to be delivered at great cost (it was all of three streets away) and we went next door to a café which was obviously full of other people who had found Steptoes too much to bear. It was slightly cleaner than Steptoes but smelled the same.

Mr Van Haagen, bowing his head towards the straw, sucked the dark coffee upwards into his mouth where he let it cool. Then he tilted his head and hoped the liquid would wash down his throat unimpeded. Sometimes it worked, sometimes not. What a way to live.

Then something must have happened in there, inside the bearded neck. He spluttered and choked. I really thought this was the end; awful, awful barking. It was worse than anything Fran had ever done. I stood. Mum stood. Several other people in the café stood too and someone tried to thump him on the back.

'Don't do that!' Mum yelled. Aunty Bev had warned us about this. 'It's nothing *stuck*, it's a spasm and you'll make it worse.'

I had never seen such twisting in a neck. Gradually, in a century or two, the choking stopped and everyone sat down again.

Mr Van Haagen spoke. 'I've had enough. Can we go?'

'Yes, I'm sorry,' said Mum. Sorry for what? Was it her fault he nearly choked to death?

I wheeled him out through the swirling floor of the carpark; the tarmac alive with whooshing leaves, banging cans, flipping crisp packets, somersaulting newspapers and hinged hamburger boxes which I'm sure were partly responsible for the hole in the sky which was causing this windstorm. Sorry, I mean 'blustery conditions'. Tomorrow they'll be calling this a hurricane but right now it's not.

'Put your head down,' I shouted, but he couldn't hear me above the din of refuse, above the orchestra of discarded packaging dancing around his wheels.

The only stable thing in this shifting world was his wheelchair, and I clung on to it. Mum clung on to me.

The journey home was not long but frightening. The wind was becoming serious: the town hovered and trembled like a duvet you have to shake down because the feathers have all gathered at the wrong end. Aunty Bev's ancient Wisteria had given up clinging to her front wall and was down around the front door and all her wallflowers were ripped out of the earth and huddled up against the bay window.

You always see yourself as soon as you enter Aunty Bev's house because facing you is a full–length mirror. You can also sometimes see part of the hall, though I don't know how. Once, soon after the installation of this mirror she had run down from the shower, clutching a towel to her bosom to answer the door. It was a candidate for the local election and he stood talking for ages, looking over her shoulder all the time. Only when he had gone did she turn and realise he had been gazing at her naked bottom for a good ten minutes, for she was only protecting her front from view. It's as well to check behind you, isn't it – there might be another point of view.

I wondered what was going through Mr Van Haagen's mind as I pushed him back into this hall. In the mirror was just an old man in a wheelchair, with a nodding head.

Chapter 22

TRYING TO DO THE SAMBA

Aunty Bev was glad to see us. I think she thought we ought not to have ventured out in what *she* had the wisdom to call force ten gales. Radio Solent was on in the kitchen and reporting cars crushed beneath falling trees all along the south coast.

'I hope Miles is being careful,' said Mum. Go on, I thought, go for it Aunty, say something horrid about him, now's your chance. She could have said, "hope he's not" or something. Instead she just said, 'Yes. Tell me about the furniture.'

Naturally my every other thought was Sunil. I was expecting him any minute now. Mum had no more clients that day and even the smell of something like scones baking could not tempt me to stay.

Mum took me home, but dropped me off and went back to Aunty Bev's. She too had 'things to do' and might need me later. Presumably this had to do with dining rooms and Miss Richardson, who was still waiting in her flat.

This meant I was about to be alone with a male person not related to me for the first time ever! Naturally I had not found it necessary, or convenient, to tell her about Sunil's visit. It had crossed my mind that she might find out (like she had about the footspa – somehow) but then, I could always say he'd just happened to call round, and what could I do? I'm not usually sneaky like this, but I could see no point in creating problems.

''Bye, Mum.'

''Bye, darling. Try to do some washing up for me, will you?'

'Course I will. 'Bye!' Normally I would have laughed at the very idea, but it seemed the *least* I could do, under the circumstances.

I had time to clear up my room – the Final Frontier of the Mess Galaxy as Dad once called it, and was just starting last night's washing up when the doorbell rang. It was Sunil – in school uniform and crash helmet!

It wasn't bad as uniforms go: in fact it was pretending to be a grey suit with only the school tie announcing that the wearer was a privileged Grammar School boy. But any uniform demotes the wearer – I mean, takes a few years off you. He looked like a tall twelve year old.

A beautiful one, though. As well as his schoolbag, he was carrying a stack of records under his arm. He had taken me at my word about the Samba! Or wanted to look as if he had.

We moved chairs around and rolled back the sitting room carpet and put a record on Dad's ancient turntable – you actually have to place the needle on the record yourself! Ah, the Samba.

Sunil took off his jacket and I buckled on my shoes and we danced.

'This floor's like concrete,' said Sunil after a few laps as my mother calls it.

'It is concrete, with thin boards on top,' I said. Most people don't realise this – that a dancer needs the floor to dance also. The floor must move with you. An unyielding floor murders the feet.

'Why is that?' he asked. I couldn't understand the question. To me to ask *why* the floor was concrete was like the question 'why cows?' or 'how the sky?'. The floor was just the floor.

'The whole house is concrete, probably,' I said, floundering.

'Except the windows,' he said. We both giggled.

'I suppose you have your own dance floor in your bedroom?' I said meaning him to laugh and deny it, as if I'd asked him whether he had his own cinema or jet engine.

'Yes, we've converted one of the garages,' he said, quite seriously. I'm sorry to say I haven't Fran's *speed* with the retorts, or I could have made some clever remark about the extravagance of having *two* garages when there were people forced to live in cardboard boxes in London. Instead I just felt rather peeved to have had my floor insulted,

160

unyielding though it was, and pulled myself away to go to the kitchen for lunch.

'Let me,' said Sunil, 'I'm not allowed to do *anything* in the kitchen at home.'

'Why not?' I feared I was about to hear something horrid about the housekeeper or some other servant doing everything, the sort of thing my parents, not to mention Fran, could tease me with forever.

'Should I so much as fill the kettle, one of my sisters rushes forward to do it for me. It's not that they think they must and I shouldn't because I've asked them about this, it's so our parents will see that they are *busy*. Industrious. Indian girls are obsessed with being busy all the time. If they watch television they must sew also, if they play chess, they must peel vegetables too. They never do just one thing, and my parents praise them for this.'

'Well, I have no such problems. Please go ahead and make whatever you like here. Make a four course dinner if you want. I shall sit and do absolutely nothing.' If either of my parents were to come in now, I shouldn't be able to do anything – I'd have been strangled!

I smiled sweetly, and watched. I let the indulgent look of a mother who watches a child make a mess of something she could easily do herself spread over my face. In fact, I do know where everything is in my kitchen because neither of my parents produce a whole meal without a lot of encouragement and assistance.

161

In fact, Home Economics is the one lesson I always pay attention in – I know my very survival depends on it.

So he began to hunt all over the kitchen in a pretend frenzy, saying, "Ah, tins!" or, "Ah, cutlery!" as if he had discovered gold. It made me laugh.

'I don't do Home Ec,' he finally admitted, having gathered together tins of soup and rice pudding on the draining board, 'I opted for Technical Drawing instead.'

'Ah well,' I said, 'you could probably draw us a lovely lunch then.'

The phone rang. I reached over for it, expecting Mum. It was unmistakably the Foul One. Sunil must have seen the dismay on my face because he stopped his fooling, became serious and sat down next to me.

'Geraldine. So glad to have caught you in at last. Could I speak to your mother?' I moved the earpiece so Sunil could hear her too. Our cheeks were almost touching.

'No. She isn't here. I'll take a message.'

'Well, now I have a place for Miss Richardson in Pine Haven Nursing Home as arranged and you and your mother can transfer her any time from now on. I have told her to be prepared. Now would be best. All right?'

'No.'

'What?'

Miss Richardson is not going into any Nursing

Home. Ever. I've decided.'

'But Geraldine, it isn't up to you. It isn't even in your mother's jurisdiction. You know that. We have decided. She has to go.' There was a pause. In the pause I could feel her trying to force me into submission. I looked at Sunil and he smiled at me.

'Nope,' I said, 'no way.'

'Geraldine, what on earth's the matter with you?'

'With me? Nothing. But I'm not giving in.' I heard an intake of breath and breathing like Mr Van Haagen, rasping and difficult.

'Perhaps I have overtaxed you and your mother a bit, sending you out to Exmouth Road like that. I can tell you've had a hard time. But decisions have been taken, arrangements have been made, and we have to abide by them.'

'I'll pass on that message, Miss Fowles. Goodbye.' And I hung up. Hung up! How did I dare?

'You are a champion, Geraldine,' said Sunil, 'but who is this Miss Richardson?'

Oh God, Miss Richardson. The wind might be tearing the world apart, but hers was already torn. Miss Fowles had warned her to 'be prepared' and she might be despairing of us even now.

I explained it quickly to Sunil, but while I was doing so something must have happened out there in the storm-filled afternoon because when I picked up the telephone again to phone Mum at Aunty Bev's the signal had gone. Just silence.

'Oh no, we'll have to go there somehow,' I said,

going to the window.

'On the radio they said only essential journeys should be undertaken,' said Sunil, coming with me to the window. Outside was his scooter, with a spare helmet attached to it. It was leaning against the garage wall.

I did wonder whether Sunil had ever taken any risks in his life. Then I realised that he had come here in the storm. But he seemed so unwilling to venture out with me in the storm on what was after all a rather harmless little scooter. It wasn't as if it were a giant Yamaha, the sort grown men race around on from one hospital to another with fresh kidneys in the courier box – it was the sort of vehicle your mother might take shopping.

'It's all backroads, no traffic, and the storm can't be *that* bad,' I said, sounding like my dad, I thought.

We went into the hall and without saying anything we put on our coats and gloves and I locked the front door and we went out bent in half to make headway in the wind, towards the vehicle.

'It's not very stable,' he shouted, holding the scooter at arms' length, steadying it in the wind. I must admit the turmoil of the weather outside mirrored my own turbulence inside: I felt almost at home in it.

'Never was a journey more essential,' I shouted back, 'Miss Richardson is in mortal danger.' I could tell he was enjoying the drama of it, though at the same time realising the idiocy of going out at all in this storm.

We seated ourselves on the bike and Sunil kickstarted it. 'Hang on to me!' he shouted. I didn't really need any encouragemnt to wrap my arms around him. Just as we turned into the wind, down the drive, a taxi pulled into it, with a very old lady in the back. It was Miss Richardson waving at us.

Chapter 23

LULL BEFORE THE STORM

The taxi driver was full of apologies, but insisted that she did have this address *written down* on a piece of paper, as if that gave her every right to be here with her many boxes, various suitcases, flute, wheelchair and plants. I don't know what she'd said to him, or how she'd persuaded him to carry all her stuff *and* her wheelchair into the car, but he seemed to be under the impression that she was a relative of ours and a bit gaga.

He and Sunil carried her into the house because the wheelchair was on the roof rack, and I helped hump everything else in. I knew it wasn't really what we'd been expecting to happen, but any uneasiness I felt then was swamped by feelings of doing a *good* thing, rescuing someone. Also – what else could I do? Sunil, too, was so obliging, so welcoming. He and Miss Richardson (who had even remembered his *name*!) were firm friends in under a minute.

Then the taxi driver went and stood over her in

the armchair in the sitting room for payment. She tipped him handsomely: several week's pocket money for the likes of me.

I shut the door. Leaves and debris had blown into the hall and settled around the boxes and suitcases dumped there. In the stillness, I thought. I tried to think positively. At least Miss Richardson was safe now and her being here was surely only temporary. I think I had imagined that things would sort themselves out at the weekend, by magic.

I walked into the sitting room. Sunil had rolled back the carpet and rearranged the furniture almost right. He excused himself with an elaborate bow to go and make the tea. Miss Richardson was sitting in my father's chair as if she had always been there. She smiled up at me as I approached and said, 'Geraldine, forgive this intrusion.'

You're not intruding,' I said.

'I am. You were just about to ride off into the sunset with your young man. I shattered a romantic moment of the first order.'

'Oh no, he isn't my young man. Not the way you mean. We were just dancing. Then the Foul One phoned and we thought we ought to go and find my mum, to rescue you.'

'But now you don't need rescuing,' said Sunil, appearing with the best tray at the door.

Then it hit me – I would need rescuing when Dad got home and found her here, installed in his chair. He would be furious. I'd done something which required permission without it. Whenever I'd done that before, I'd been in real trouble. It is where my Dad says he *draws the line*. And what's more, I could already foresee with a sort of vague inner terror, that somehow this transgression would be linked to my having *sneaked* a boy in without anyone knowing – for that was bound to come out too.

'Oh, no,' I said.

'What?' they both said, together.

'I think I'll be in terrible trouble about all this.' I pointed vaguely at them both and the cases in the hall. How to explain without hurting anyone's feelings? How to say that Mum and I hadn't really made any firm arrangement yet for Miss Richardson or that I hadn't actually cleared it with anyone for Sunil to be here? I couldn't. So I said, 'I must get in touch with Mum immediately.'

'Telephone?' said Miss Richardson.

'The lines are down,' said Sunil, moving to the window.

'No, you can't go out in this!' said Miss Richardson. She looked agitated.

'We'll have to,' I said. 'It'll be all right. It's only blustery conditions.' I tried to sound reassuring like the weatherpersons on children's television, or my Dad during a nuclear holocaust, when I'm sure he'd be offering people comforting cups of tea!

Well it didn't reassure anyone, but we went. Miss Richardson looked pale and worried as we left and Sunil was putting on a brave face.

Chapter 24

THE ACCIDENT

The late afternoon was turning into a disaster movie. It would be brill fun to sit in a plush velvet armchair with a bag of caramel popcorn and watch it on the screen. Especially with Sunil's arm on my shoulder. But being out in it was less than fun. Even having both arms around Sunil wasn't really romantic because if I'd let go, I'd have spun off onto the road and my kidneys would have become available for the dispatch riders to deliver.

This thought, the possibility of instant death, rather filled my brain. There was no room for anything else, though I did wonder at the route we were taking. Finally Sunil shouted to me, 'I CAN'T GO LEFT!' and I understood. We were way off course.

In fact we were in the middle of the area my father likes to use for beginners, where he says Bungaloiditis has broken out. Just rows and rows of bungalows with huge picture windows facing the sea. One or two had shattered and people were nailing boards up to replace them.

Naturally, we didn't see the orange ticker tape across the road – but we *heard* it because the wind was playing it like a guitar. A man wearing a construction worker's helmet, one of many, ran towards us as we stopped.

'WHAT'S THE MEANING OF THIS?'

He was furious with Sunil. I don't know whether the fact that he was endangering *my* life or his own was the worse crime, but the punishment was clear: he insisted that Sunil park and leave the scooter.

'Walk!' he shouted to us, trotting away. So we started to walk and then run away from a partially crushed house they were shoring up. Holding hands. Well, even in a dire emergency you can't help thinking this is a brilliant opportunity to hold hands! Fortunately it was mostly downhill. We had to dodge strange objects which flew around our feet: toys which belonged in sandpits, tea towels, underwear with pegs still attached.

Several tall thin Scots pines were down along the exposed sea coast area we were running through. At last the road dipped and we made our way downhill to Aunty Bev's where we burst through the front door and almost ran into them, Aunty dressed in her camelhair overcoat and headscarf, Mum in her awful anorak.

'Aunty,' I panted, 'emergency. The Foul One has struck! Miss Richardson is . . .' I couldn't get my words out. Mum was staring behind me at Sunil.

Aunty Bev said, 'We have an emergency too. Your Mum found this note.' She showed me a scrap of paper with the following words written on one side:

HAVE GONE OUT – LOVE E & E XXX

'And the police are too busy to take this seriously, it seems,' she added.

'Yes. Mum – you remember Sunil?' I said, stupidly. I didn't know what to say – I was dreading her asking him what he was doing there.

'Of course I do. Hello, Sunil.'

'Perhaps I can be of assistance, Mrs Budd?' Then a kind of indoor storm erupted. Everyone, including Mr Van Haagen, said very loudly that *they* would find the twins, so it wasn't a question of who would stay behind with Mr Van Haagen but of how we would all proceed without the car which was thought too dangerous by everyone. Sunil solved that by declaring that he would do the pushing and the front door was suddenly open in the hall and a whole bush came in the front door and a picture twisted off the wall. We all trotted out – Mum and Aunty Bev in the lead, and Sunil pushing Mr Van Haagen. I tried to keep up with Sunil.

The air outside was as loud as a steel band in full throttle so my voice was drowned. I hadn't said all the things I'd braved life and limb to come and say, nor had I explained Sunil's presence, but somehow none of it mattered now. We were a *posse*: finding the daffy old sisters was our whole and only aim. Things were still flying through the air before us.

171

Impossible things like quilted peg bags in the shape of hearts with looped handles. How would people ever get these things back?

As we settled into a jog – Sunil now in front with the chair going a good lick, with a tailwind, uphill towards cliffs along the sea's edge – I was determined to give them at least the bones of what was happening.

Isn't it strange how shouting alters your vocabulary? Everything becomes rather *tabloid* suddenly, almost low-grade. In real life, at talking pitch, I would never have said, 'MISS RICHARDSON HAS DONE A FLIT.' But that's what I said. It sounded like a newspaper headline rather than a piece of information.

Their astonishment would have been satisfying were it not that the very next moment, having trotted over the (deserted) Southbourne Crossroads, we turned into the Overcliff, a long road running along the top of the cliff and saw the twins in the distance. Aunty Bev shouted but the wind took her voice and the twins carried on, regardless.

We ran. Mr Van Haagen gripped the arm of his chair with one hand and waved his hat about in the air with the other, as if urging on horses.

Before we caught up with them, we saw them turn and walk into the road to cross over to the playground on the cliff top just as a furniture removal van hurtled past towards them.

So often in dreams reality thumbs its nose at me

by slowing down just when I most need to run or shout or warn someone – the floor becomes toffee, the air wool, the voice dead – but it doesn't often happen when I'm awake. It did then. We all froze and I wanted to shut my eyes.

Mr Van Haagen rose unassisted and quickly from his chair and from somewhere inside him came a megaphone of a voice, not his, which shouted through the wind, 'EDNA! EDITH!'

They turned, saw us, and started back, smiling. The spell was broken and we all ran forward to help them. The furniture van, the driver braking just in the nick of time, skidded off the road onto the grass clifftop, where it uncoupled itself sideways around a metal slide, burst open at the end and, hanging over the edge of the clifftop, sprayed its contents over the cliff down onto the beach.

Chapter 25

WHAT HE WANTED

Maybe the wind caught Mr Van Haagen, causing him to lose his balance, damaged in any case. Maybe he was weakened by the unusual physical activities we had put him through, or it may simply have been that in achieving at last 'an heroic act', he deliberately overreached himself and gave in to death.

What I saw at any rate was that he smiled triumphantly when the sisters were rescued, spread out his arms like someone removing his tie after a long spell at work, twisted round and fell hard and suddenly onto the pavement, hitting his head. Nothing broke his fall and he must have died instantly, for Aunty Bev found no pulse a moment later and if anyone could she would have.

It was the death he had wanted. The heroic death, almost a battlefield death. There was nothing gruesome about it – it was dignified and lovely. Aunty Bev covered his face, which was quite handsome without any spasm, with her silk scarf, tucking in the long white hair to avoid the wind. But the wind would keep catching it, pulling it away. It was no more use than a piece of dried grass.

I felt my own knees give way and sank down beside him, where I sat, too upset to cry, until they came to carry him away.

His had been a big life. There were whole passages of it no one knew about. Whole episodes, in Holland, I should have asked about. Whole terrible reasons for being here, maybe a whole life abandoned for this one, now gone. None of us really knew him. We knew his spasms and his swallowing problem and his slight accent amused us. My aunty cared for him, fed him, washed him even. But we didn't know him. Now it is too late to tell him we did really care about who he was. Too late to say I sort of loved him.

Chapter 26

ALL CHANGE

Although there were real ambulances and members of the general public were arriving from nowhere with saws to free people, there were no real police. This was because all police had been called out already to deal with the enormous number of accidents all over the south coast. Our little collision was just one of many that day.

Because there were as yet no real police, it was chaos, and ambulancemen were appointing members of the public to act as constables and keep people away. Hence while rescue was going on fifty yards away from us, we were being kept away by a woman in a blue anorak who would sooner die than let us catch a glimpse of anything going on over by the playground.

Other people were carried carefully across the playground and put in ambulances and whisked away, but I'm sorry to say none of them mattered to me then at all. Only Mr Van Haagen, lying peacefully in a silent ambulance waiting for a free driver mattered. I didn't want to leave him alone with strangers. I suppose that's always the way: if a train crashed and hundreds of people died, you'd only mourn your own friends.

Finally, the police arrived. Mr Van Haagen was driven off, without us. The police wanted *witnesses* – someone who had actually seen what had happened. I heard Mum volunteering herself as the *only* eyewitness and agreeing to give her version of it. She left for the station.

I felt I needed someone to take care of me. Aunty Bev had a wheelchair and the twins to get home. Little did she know that she already had Miss Richardson to collect from my house. I thought I'd wait to break this to her. There was so much going on.

Sunil appeared with his scooter, so we parted politely under Aunty Bev's watchful eye. In fact, we shook hands!

Trouble was, we had no transport. In the end, one of the policemen gave us a lift home, together with wheelchair and twins, confused and distraught blaming each other for causing the accident.

I had never noticed before how weird they looked. They must be in their eighties, quite thin and frail and their hair really is dry and white like straw, all wind-blown. They are, like slightly animated identical corn dollies, no more. The sort of thing that comes to life only in dreams.

From their account you couldn't really work out

what had happened. Only that eventually they decided to go out into the hurricane and got lost. Then they started weeping and said they would give anything to have Mr Van Haagen back again.

The policeman who helped us to shift everything from the car to Aunty Bev's, including the twins, refused a cup of tea, and left.

The twins went slowly up the stairs in silence and we heard their door shut. Then a loud thumping began, interspersed with sounds of whooshing. It was as if the hurricane, now dying down outside, was concentrated in their room.

'Are they all right?' I asked.

'Yes. They're making something big,' Aunty said.

Then we went into the kitchen.

'Of course, I'll have to pretend to be cross with them, even though I know nothing is really their fault. So that they won't feel guilty. God, it's like having children!' she said, putting on the kettle.

'Only worse. They never grow up,' I said.

'That's right, they just die.' Then she looked up at me as if to say 'what have I said?'

'Like Mr Van Haagen!' I burst into tears.

'Cheer up, Geraldine!' she said, 'it's not the end of the world. Mr Van Haagen was very old and always uncomfortable, and had the best sudden death you could hope for, almost heroic. And now I've got room for your Miss Richardson.' So, she'd brought it up herself.

Maybe it was all the excitement, or maybe it was because I'd had no lunch, I don't know, but I started to cry hysterically then. I wept and wept. I could hear myself blurting out things about my dad having ruined her life: things I had never meant to say.

She ooched up to me on the pew and said, 'I don't know what you've heard, but let me say, it never pays to listen at keyholes: you always get a twisted version of the truth. Nobody ruined my life. My life is my own. I never wanted to marry, or have my own children. Then Bella had you and you were a demanding baby. Not bad, just demanding and I was thrilled to share the burden. Your mum and I used to argue all the time as children, but suddenly that was all over – we could share you, love you together.

'You took your first steps in my house, did your first dance for me. I've had all the advantages of a daughter of my own without any of the disadvantages. When you had trouble with them, you came to me. I never had to discipline you or criticise your friends or tell you when to be in by. What more could an aunt ask for? There's no bitterness in me, Geraldine, none at all. And now, where have you hidden Miss Richardson?'

We laughed.

'She's at our house.'

'In her wheelchair?'

'No, in Dad's armchair.'

'Then she must be dying for a wee.'

'I didn't think of that – oh, quick!'

* * *

So Aunty and I went in her car to collect Miss Richardson. The hurricane was dying down at last. Every tree on every road seemed to have at least one broken branch hanging by a thread. Everything looked exhausted. Hunger gripped me like a stomach ache.

Miss Richardson was very glad to see us, and while Aunty was loading up her boxes, whispered to me, 'You should have warned me. What a formidable woman!'

'No,' I said, defending her, 'she is just a very fashionable person. You'll love her.' I know the way she dresses makes people think she's frightening, or in some way judging you for your shabbiness. But it isn't true – she just has *style*.

Of course, Aunty didn't need to put the wheelchair on the roof-rack because her rear seat flipped down (at the touch of a button) to make a huge area at the back. She said she would put Miss Richardson into the chair first at the other end, so she would not need my help.

I was glad. I'd had enough, and I was starving.

When they'd gone, I made myself a sandwich from two crusts left in the breadbin and honey. Then I drank a whole pint of milk and felt normal again.

Which is more than could be said for the house. A week ago I wouldn't even have noticed the leaves and twigs strewn on the hall floor or the fact that the sitting room furniture was all in the wrong place. Or rather, I'd have noticed, but I'd have said to myself, hope Mum straightens it all up soon.

But that was last week.

I vacuumed the hall and rearranged the lounge and washed up and generally did the sort of job on the house which Miss Fowles would expect of someone in her employ. Then I sat down in the kitchen as it got dark and began to feel elated.

I might have misunderstood a lot of things and made fusses where there was no need, but my Work Experience had ended, and everything had turned out so *well*, apart from Mr Van Haagen, but Aunty was right – I must learn to see that as a blessing.

I wanted, badly, to share this with someone. I tried the phone again. Working. I phoned Fran.

Chapter 27

FRAN

'Mrs Goode? Could I speak to Fran?'

'No, you can't. She's far too ill to come to the phone.'

'Why, what's happened?'

'I think she overdid it at the dance. I had my doubts. I should have been firm. She wasn't able to go to work today. She's resting.'

'Can I visit?'

'She can have visitors, but only for a short time. Say, ten minutes.'

'I'll be right there. I'll come now.'

So it's all my fault. Sunil and I danced her into an illness. We made her ill. On the other hand, is she never to have any fun? Perhaps it was Thursday's pension day at the post office which overtaxed her, not the dance?

I had to take a bus.

The bus took ages. There were diversions

everywhere, presumably to avoid wind damage, fallen trees, and stranded cars.

Also, Fran lives on the other side of town. I know why this is. We did it in Geography with the grotty Miss Carter: when they invented our town, in the Victorian era, the rich people took all the land by the sea, the high ground, and built themselves mansions with big gardens overlooking the bay. Then humbler homes were needed for the grocers and tradespeople, so smaller houses closer together (like ours) sprang up on the roads leading to the clifftop. Then very small terraced two-up two-down houses for the families of the servants of the rich coast dwellers had to be built on the northernmost outskirts of the town. Fran lived about as far north as you can, before the New Forest starts.

The odd thing is, I had never been there. Fran had been to my house many times, but we usually met in town. So there was never any need for me to go to Fran's. Just as well because my Dad said he didn't really want me to go to an 'area like that'.

So, I'd better not let him know that I came here. It's not lying: it just won't come up, I hope.

The road was quiet. The first house in it was a corner shop. I nipped in and bought some chocolate mints. Then I counted to find the house. Mrs Goode answered the door. She didn't look pleased to see me. I wasn't surprised. I don't think Fran's mother likes me at all anyway, and at the moment I am the bad influence who made her ill. She thinks.

Fran was lying in the bottom bunk in the front room and didn't open her eyes when I entered.

The room was a bedroom, but it should have been the lounge, being downstairs and at the front of the house. Also, it was clearly not solely *her* room, for the top bunk was messy and the walls covered with Ninja Turtle posters which I knew couldn't be Fran's. Her brother must *share* this room.

I could imagine Mum coming here as the Home Help and saying 'soon get this sorted out,' and whizzing around picking up all the dirty socks, comics, mugs, and mess.

'Fran,' I said, 'it's me, Geraldine.' Then she stirred and looked most surprised.

I didn't know you were coming,' she said.

'Well, here I am.' I gave her the mints.

'How kind.' She didn't seem the same person. She seemed less, somehow. Not what I'd expected. I think I'd expected to find the usual, frothy Fran, only lying down. I could see now that there just wouldn't be a stream of amusing comments issuing from her sickbed.

So I sat down on the edge of the bed (there was nowhere else) and told her, blow by blow, about my day. I don't think I'd ever talked so continuously before to anyone. It seemed to distract her. She smiled in places, let her mouth drop open at others. When I'd finished, with the transfer of Miss Richardson to her new home, she said, 'And to think, all that going on out there while I lay here.'

'Yes, why are you here? Is this a bedroom or what?' I suppose it was a rude question, but I asked it nonetheless.

'My mum rents out the upstairs bedroom, to someone we call The Ancient Mariner, and sleeps in the other room. My brother and I share this room.'

Her brother had the lion's share, too, since *his* things were strewn over ninety per cent of it, while Fran seemed to own one small doorless cupboard in which hung her school uniform, the culottes and one dress.

When Fran had called our house lovely, I'd thought she was just being polite.

'Written your Report?' asked Fran.

'Report?'

'Surely you haven't forgotten.' No, I hadn't forgotten. I think the idea of having to write a report about my Work Experience Week had been so frightening that I'd dismissed it from my mind.

'Due in Monday,' said Fran.

'No doubt you've finished yours?'

'Yes, I only had four days to report, and that was standing behind a counter all day.'

'I thought all human life passed in front of that grill?' She laughed. Then coughed. Her mother appeared at the door.

'Time's up,' she said.

'Oh, please. I've only just got here,' I said.

'You could use your word processor,' said Fran.

'Fran, we're not *that* rich! We haven't got a computer.'

'Oh, I thought you had. Well, I'm sure Sunil has. Most boys his age have to put up with a pushbike. Phone him up and ask.'

'What a good idea,' I said. Fran smiled, wickedly. She would be much better at conducting an affair than me. I only hope she gets the chance one day.

'You really must go now,' said Mrs Goode.

On the way out, I turned to her and said, 'I'm ever so sorry about this.' She opened the door and said, 'Oh, don't worry. This happens. As if life isn't hard enough. This happens.'

I felt sad on the journey home. In front of me on the bus two women in headscarves were talking loudly. One was telling the other about an incident at the Front earlier that day. She told her companion that the wind was so high that the entire contents of someone's house were swept over the cliff and into the sea. Normally I would have laughed.

My road was dark. All the street lights were out. I made my way home by touch. I know the walls. I've done this walk from the bus a million times.

Two minutes after I arrived home, Mum and Dad (whom she had phoned from the station) came back. They had brought two things with them – fish and chips (still hot!) and a sealed envelope from Miss Fowles to Miss Carter – her Report on me, which Mum had been given along with her wages which she'd just collected without resigning.

Never did fish and chips taste so wonderful.

They must have assumed I'd been here all the

time, because they didn't say 'where were you?' or anything. Of course, I didn't tell them. Neither did I try to explain to Mum why Sunil had been with me – the death of Mr Van Haagen had eclipsed all that. Dad handed me the envelope and they went off to bed.

Naturally as soon as they had gone to bed I steamed it open. I've never done it before, but it's quite easy. The hard bit is getting the kettle to keep boiling, since it wants to switch itself off when it boils.

This is what she said about me:

Dear Miss Carter,

As you know I was happy to accept Geraldine Budd on a week's placement as a Work Experience student, even at extremely short notice. I was assured by her mother that she would be both diligent and responsible, and assumed, wrongly I now see, that she would not have been recommended by her school, were she not capable of the work.

The very first day of her accompanying her mother on her rounds of the Long Term Elderly, I received a complaint from a Mrs Gaitskill, a lady in her eighties, about the standard of work. The very next day that lady had a bad accident, and Geraldine was delegated to telephone me. It was an abrupt call, and I detected that the girl was panicking unnecessarily.

On the Thursday I was obliged to visit another

187

elderly lady to assess her for entry to a nursing home. Geraldine behaved most obstructively during the interview, and it was only the following day, when I telephoned to say that I had obtained a place for this lady in a nursing home and required that she and her mother effect the removal, that the full weight of her rebelliousness struck me. She refused, outright, to comply with my instructions.

I can only say it was chance which intervened in such a way that her refusal did not result in any ill befalling the client, not responsible action. I am sure it is not unreasonable to say that I am glad Geraldine's week with Social Services is over, and am unlikely ever to accept another student under the same circumstances.

Yours sincerely,

M. Fowles.

Director, Home Help.

Dear Diary:

Today Mr Van Haagen died. I saved his life once. I am trying to see it as a blessing — now Miss Richardson has somewhere to live (his room at Aunty's). I wish Miss Fowles would catch a fatal disease and die.

Chapter 28

MY OWN REPORT

I was determined that at least she wouldn't have the last word on the matter. My Report would be the most spectacular piece of writing the school had ever received in this context. Of course I am no idiot, and well aware that nothing I write *personally* could be spectacular.

So on Saturday morning I enlisted the help of both Sunil and (the much recovered) Fran, not to mention Sunil's word processor. Fran had been right about that – he did indeed have his own.

Mum drove me to Fran's house. We reassured her mother that Fran would do nothing more strenuous than sit at a keyboard, so she was allowed to come. Then Mum took us to Sunil's house, and we began.

First I showed them Miss Fowles' Report, which I hadn't resealed yet.

'Now we know what we're up against,' said Sunil.

'I admire her style,' said Fran, 'pen like a scalpel.'

I said things out loud. Fran rephrased them. Sunil typed onto the screen. We were quite a team. After an hour of this, his little sister brought us drinks of her own invention (pink lemonade with blue ice cubes) and biscuits she had made in the shape of the suits of cards. No doubt she had knitted a glove and played chess at the same time.

'The trick is,' said Sunil, 'for it not to *seem* that you steamed open her report, read it and answered it. This has to answer all her criticisms as if by coincidence.'

'You'd make a good criminal,' said Fran.

I ended up writing the report myself really – with advice from Sunil and Fran at crucial moments. It was a work of art, lingering at some length on my lifesaving.

Sunil printed it out in a bold large font and I went and sat on the window seat overlooking the bay to read it. Yes, it's one of those mansions. In the background someone was playing an electronic keyboard with solo styleplay on, so that each note trembled a little before moving on.

I read.

EPILOGUE

The cork noticeboard at the end of Sunil's converted garage has the full story — after all, Mr Van Haagen was a hero and local geriatric — the most popular combination you could be here in our town. The newspaper photograph showed him as a young man at the top and the giant raffia wings the twins had laid on his coffin at the bottom. The newspaper had even unearthed a war story about his escape from Holland in 1941 to add flavour to his heroic death.

And sitting next to it in bright red — for Sunil's mother had persuaded her to abandon all drabness starting with her black dresses — sat Miss Richardson, urging us on.

She thinks she understands our dancing. And us. We humour her of course.

In fact, I've only got to look into his eyes to know that he knows that the dancing is not just dancing.

THE END

A Selected List of Fiction from Mammoth

While every effort is made to keep prices low, it is sometimes necessary to increase prices at short notice. Mandarin Paperbacks reserves the right to show new retail prices on covers which may differ from those previously advertised in the text or elsewhere.

The prices shown below were correct at the time of going to press.

☐ 7497 0978 2	**Trial of Anna Cotman**	Vivien Alcock	£2.50
☐ 7497 0712 7	**Under the Enchanter**	Nina Beachcroft	£2.50
☐ 7497 0106 4	**Rescuing Gloria**	Gillian Cross	£2.50
☐ 7497 0035 1	**The Animals of Farthing Wood**	Colin Dann	£3.50
☐ 7497 0613 9	**The Cuckoo Plant**	Adam Ford	£3.50
☐ 7497 0443 8	**Fast From the Gate**	Michael Hardcastle	£1.99
☐ 7497 0136 6	**I Am David**	Anne Holm	£2.99
☐ 7497 0295 8	**First Term**	Mary Hooper	£2.99
☐ 7497 0033 5	**Lives of Christopher Chant**	Diana Wynne Jones	£2.99
☐ 7497 0601 5	**The Revenge of Samuel Stokes**	Penelope Lively	£2.99
☐ 7497 0344 X	**The Haunting**	Margaret Mahy	£2.99
☐ 7497 0537 X	**Why The Whales Came**	Michael Morpurgo	£2.99
☐ 7497 0831 X	**The Snow Spider**	Jenny Nimmo	£2.99
☐ 7497 0992 8	**My Friend Flicka**	Mary O'Hara	£2.99
☐ 7497 0525 6	**The Message**	Judith O'Neill	£2.99
☐ 7497 0410 1	**Space Demons**	Gillian Rubinstein	£2.50
☐ 7497 0151 X	**The Flawed Glass**	Ian Strachan	£2.99

All these books are available at your bookshop or newsagent, or can be ordered direct from the publisher. Just tick the titles you want and fill in the form below.

Mandarin Paperbacks, Cash Sales Department, PO Box 11, Falmouth, Cornwall TR10 9EN.

Please send cheque or postal order, no currency, for purchase price quoted and allow the following for postage and packing:

UK including BFPO	£1.00 for the first book, 50p for the second and 30p for each additional book ordered to a maximum charge of £3.00.
Overseas including Eire	£2 for the first book, £1.00 for the second and 50p for each additional book thereafter.

NAME (Block letters) ....

ADDRESS ....

....

☐ I enclose my remittance for ....

☐ I wish to pay by Access/Visa Card Number

Expiry Date